101 Ways
Your mother said you could die

a novel

Chris Culler

Book design by The Blue One
www.theblueone.com

ISBN: 0692308962
ISBN 13: 9780692308967
Library of Congress Control Number: 2014920993
Cullerful Imprint * Venice, California

For Pete Culler

who took the pictures, packed his passport,
and was the first of us to go.

"…Death will take care of itself. Worry about life, that needs management."

Michel de Montaigne

"It's never too late to be who you might have been."

George Eliot

101 Ways
Your Mother Said You Could Die

"Be smart choosing your friends.
Many murder victims knew their killers."

On the Amazon rainforest there are monstrous anacondas lolling in tree canopies just waiting for easy prey. There are also poison dart frogs, jaguars, and tiny lethal spiders that kill in a single heartbeat. And then there are humans. Humans are the deadliest threat of all. I listen for the crunch of footsteps outside our *caleta* and assure myself we have a gun, but actually, *he* is the one with the Walther PPK. I'm not the sort of person who says "Walther PPK" nor was I, until tonight, capable of identifying one.

Through the steady plop-plop-plop of rainwater dripping through the mangroves and the shrieks of *las chicharras* and other forest creatures warbling, ticking, prowling the night, I mull over how murder victims are often killed by people they knew, people they once trusted. Such as the man sleeping beside me, for instance, though I rationally disregard this notion. Or rather try to. Psychotherapy may have played a significant role in my functional adulthood but it hasn't entirely loosened anxiety's mental stranglehold, no matter how cognitive my thinking. They say a boa constrictor tightens its grip when you struggle.

There were the obvious yet unheeded warnings: The fleet of Mercedes; the boasts of the *sicario*; the *discoteca* inside the gated compound with its hallucinogenic *datura* and sweet intoxicating yet ultimately suffocating scent of *piñuelas* and *yarumos*. Whether I say I came willingly or claim I was abducted, I lie here now, wrapped in a shroud of mosquito netting. I should have taken the first flight home if not for a foolhardy impulse to alter my genetic nerve structure into that audacious and daring woman I have never really been and most likely never will be.

"Come live with me in the ceiba tree," he said in *that* voice.

And so, seduced by the rising temperature of the skin I live in, propelled by an impetus as prehistoric as this primordial swamp, I followed the fellow, fearing then and knowing even better now that impassioned liaisons of this sort aren't meant for those nurtured on the probability of disastrous outcomes.

We could disappear into *Lago Tarapoto* and swim with the pink dolphins and no one would ever find us, or suspect who did us in.

— —

Drought Tolerant

"Look both ways before crossing a one way street. A car could be coming from the wrong direction."

Before my Amazonian journey I went through a period when I seldom ventured beyond the three-mile radius of my bungalow in Venice, California. I rarely questioned my agoraphobic self-incarceration until one day I was set adrift by a sea change brought on by the revival of a long dormant passion. Suddenly my perspective altered on just about everything, especially courage and love.

The first instant of this transformation occurs at 3:53 a.m., when a police helicopter swoops down and around and over my house, its whacking rotor blades jolting me awake to a sudden awareness that today, for the first time in years, I will be driving the freeway. Then it comes and there's no stopping it: the shortness of breath, racing heartbeat, sense of doom. Dread spreads through my ribcage, slithers around me like a paralyzing caress. All I am is a reasonably healthy woman in the middle of a panic attack. *No biggie,* I think, but still I fail to assure myself or stop the terror.

I slip out of bed and stand at the window — just in time for the chopper's spotlight to illuminate me in its stark, unforgiving beam: An anxious woman with bed-head hair and flannel PJs in the middle years of her preciously cautious life. She may have ancestral jewels hidden in her sock drawer or a laptop on the counter, and thanks to the LAPD, it's glaringly official: Here she is, the vulnerable homeowner, a sitting duck just waiting to be robbed.

Swirling with vertigo, I creep back to bed. Winston bathes on the pillow where Charlie's head used to be. Patrick kneads tufts of feather from the quilting and Darwin gazes into my face with all the calm assurance of a Buddha, but there's no going back, no slowing the escalation of my heartbeat, though I've been counseled by experts. Panic attacks are purely a mental condition due to excess adrenaline provoked by a fight-or-flight response yet without anything specific to fight or fly from. I need merely wait for it to pass, this abrupt comprehension of my own mortality.

How is it that the daughter of the once intrepid Harry Barnes who moved his family to all parts of the world from the deserts of the Middle East to the jungles of South America, ended up fearing the 405?

According to the American Psychiatric Association's *DSM*, or *Diagnostic and Statistical Manual of Mental Disorders*, "complicated grief" lasting longer than the considered "normal" two months bereavement signifies a possible depressive anxiety disorder. One might therefore conclude that if two months of grieving is considered normal, two years places me in the certifiably crazy zone. Yet who is to say what is normal in matters of heart and passing souls? Grief can't be surgically removed nor zapped with radiation or chemo. It doesn't fall under tidy definitions such as "prolonged" or "complicated," no matter what the *DSM* might say. Charlie and Father, both of whom by pure fate died within months of each other, cannot be brought back, nor can I be airlifted to them through some magical portal in the sky.

The police helicopter makes a final sweep of the neighborhood and lifts up and away, its search over. Without my noticing (the trick is in not noticing), my heartbeat slows. Lying here in the pre-dawn silence

I assure myself that an intruder lurking like some creepy garden troll under my bougainvillea is highly unlikely as I happen to reside behind a fortress of thorny shrubs, formidable gate, and double-locked windows and doors. I've been cautioned by the best. I know the score.

~ ~

"Be careful on stairs. You could fall and break your neck."

precarious stairway leads down from my attic bedroom and I nearly slip on grass-encrusted cat vomit on the steep third step. Close call. But then, my fiercely protective mother resides a few houses down, ready like an on-duty fireman to rescue me on a moment's notice. She could discover my paraplegic body in time to rush me to the hospital then spoon-feed me the rest of my life, a truly abhorrent situation that would provide the very kind of calling she's been waiting for.

My little bungalow is swept clean like a beach in winter. There are the spare white walls, pieces of driftwood; no memorabilia or memories on the shelves, no signs of the person I was in the time of Charlie. This I reserve for the back closet where I slip into his flannel shirt, take in the remnants of his scent and glance at a picture of him grinning wide in a fire suit from a time when, driving freeways to film locations, I came into the unlikely sphere of a daring stuntman.

Barefoot, I peer through the glass pane on the front door into the blue light of early morning. I ascertain no lurking intruder, unbolt the double locks, and step out to the scent of sage rising from the cool damp earth.

My garden faces a narrow sidewalk separating the houses on my side from those across the way in what is known as the "walk streets" neighborhood. This is my refuge, my job with Magill Landscaping but five blocks away and thereby making it possible for me to avoid freeways. Until today.

At the window in the bungalow next door I see Juanita's bubble-head of white hair pass by. Up early as usual, my one hundred year-old neighbor sets up a pot for her boiled egg. She is lovely and fragile, like a Venetian glass figurine. She could shatter in an instant but until then she's delicately brilliant, and the bravest person I know. Juanita sees me through her window and waves. I wave back. Her garden is subtropical and vibrant and the antithesis of mine which, by contrast, is sustainably drought tolerant. In Juanita's little front beds, ginger plants rise to the sky, banana palms fan into fronds. Tangerines spill down from branches toward the sidewalk, ripe for picking by strangers and neighbors who are encouraged to do so. Just the other day, she planted *Meconopsis Betonicifolia*, better known as Himalayan Blue Poppy, which is not only an exotic choice but, considering it won't bloom for at least another spring, an optimistic one.

Inspired by my courageous centenarian neighbor, I repeat a mantra in my head: *I will not crash on the 405 today.*

There may be police choppers circling our rooftops, internet news flashes of revolutions, tsunamis, hurricanes and nuclear radiation; there may be oil spreading a dark warning on the wings of birds and in the ocean's whale songs portending disaster as they deepen in pitch, but we the normal carry on.

Back inside the house my phone's loud vibration on the oak surface of the dining table sounds like the precursory rumble of an earthquake. It isn't a quake, but close.

"Do you think it was another break-in?" are my mother's first words of the day.

Awakened by the early morning police helicopter, she assumes misfortune has visited someone in the neighborhood, and while she would certainly feel terrible, she's nonetheless excited by the prospect of feeling terrible.

"Try not to worry, Margaret," I say. By calling her Margaret I can be just enough amused by her peculiarities to marginally keep her from getting under my skin. "Mother" rushes through my nervous system; "Margaret" is simply an irritating friend.

"You know I just keep thinking about it."

"You could try *not* thinking about it."

Telling Mother not to think about high crime, murder and mayhem is like saying don't think of a pink elephant. The thought inflates like a giant Macy's balloon and fills every corner of her brain. To get her off this fixation I blurt out my plan to drive to Newport today and by her reaction you'd think I'd announced plans to race in the Indy 500.

"Oh, Mira, no! When was the last time you drove the 405?"

"We're setting up planters for a wedding party," I say, "We're already overwhelmed with the tour, so this time Magill asked me to deliver them."

Ever since my planter arrangements appeared in a popular photo spread in *Garden Design*, I have become Magill's second-in-command.

"I'll drive you," says my eighty-two year old mother. The notion of having to ride beside Mother clutching the steering wheel with cars zooming past us at nearly twice the speed is so laughingly terrifying it quickens my heartbeat to the level of an antihistamine overdose.

"No thanks, Mom."

"I'll be right over."

"I thought I heard myself say no."

"To feed your cats."

"I'm not going away on vacation. I'm just driving to Orange County."

Having moved from the Midwest suburbs to ostensibly look after me, Margaret needs to feel needed. And I *did* need her for a while. I was drowning in grief, removed from the world around me and hunkered down in my house, but a dread of freeways is not a good thing if you live in Southern California. It makes arriving on the set of a downtown shoot near impossible, and after a while you don't know if it's the speed of the drivers or a loss of confidence in the job you're driving to, but gradually you allow that livelihood and career and most of the friends in your former field to drift away. Dear mother arrived with her cats, found a reasonably priced rental nearby, moved in, and harangued and pushed me into at least stepping outside into my garden. I then found a job in my own neighborhood, swapping out dressing sets at distant film locations for dressing planter pots instead.

Yet as I've regained my bearings in recent months I've begun to sense Mother's discontent. It was advantageous to her, having a "sick" child, but I am not a child, although I *am* her daughter, and being Margaret's daughter entails a constant gentle pulling away from her overpowering desire to alternately protect and terrorize. After all, how can she protect me from the mean bad world if I'm also not terrorized by it in some way?

"Never Feel Safe" was the memorable chapter heading from a book Mother once gave me when I left for college titled, *Career Girl, Watch Out*. Never feel safe, the book said, no matter where you are. And so I've done precisely that, remained on the lookout for imminent danger always, owning that readiness like my own name printed in indelible ink onto the waistband of my undies before heading to summer camp.

—　～

— ~

*"Don't drive behind a flatbed truck
carrying appliances.
A refrigerator could fall off the back and slam
into your windshield."*

— ~

 feed the cats, and have just finished brewing a pot of Mocha Java
 when my phone rings again.

"I knew she'd call you," I say to my sister Rosie.

"Can you believe she wants me to talk sense into you?"

I see Rosie at the wheel of her Prius, her hair fashionably chopped,
a pair of reading glasses hanging from her neck. At first glance no one
would guess we are sisters. Her hair is auburn while mine is streaky
blond. She is strong of will, contending with knee surgery and back
pain, while I persistently worry about being afflicted with various ail-
ments that have yet to be diagnosed. But what we have in common is our

continued impulse to nurture the illusion that our childhood traveling the world within our family's dysfunction has kept us in solidarity. These days Rosie polishes her Ann Arbor house into an antique showpiece, brilliantly diagnoses the most baffling cases, saves lives, produces *cordon bleu* meals, drives her seven-year-old son to play dates and bullies her husband into getting off the couch, but this doesn't mean she can alter that persistent tug of worry and dissatisfaction branded into our nervous systems.

I want to warn her about the hazards of maneuvering through Michigan roads during an early May hailstorm and talking on her cellphone to me, but this could provoke a comparison to Mother, and the worst thing one of us can say to the other is "you sound like Mom."

"You are aware that by having told her," Rosie says, "You inadvertently asked her permission."

No one can push my buttons like Rosie. I may have been given the consolation prize of "emotional intelligence," but Rosie is emotionally strategic.

"Believe me, I didn't ask her permission. Everyone's too busy so I'm making the delivery. This is a must-do."

"You'll be fine," says the doc in an auspiciously cheerful tone, "First you get back on the freeway, then in a couple weeks you'll fly back here with Mother!"

"Are you kidding? Fly with Mom?"

Flying is not for the sisters raised on the precept:

> *"Letting both my daughters fly on the same plane*
> *Is like putting all your eggs in one basket."*

Whenever Father was transferred to a new country Mother relocated us by train or ocean liner, and when we flew back to the States on our own as teenagers, she had us take separate flights, her logic being that if an airplane's going to crash with one of her daughters she'd at least have one left. Father went along with this. Would *you* want to be responsible for the deaths of *both* of your children?

"Pop a Xanax," Rosie says, "I prescribed Mom plenty. Call Dr. I if you have to."

"We'll see."

"I'll make the reservations."

"Hold on —"

"Don't you want to see Jonathan? It's been two years!"

"I don't think I'm ready to get on a plane with her."

"You've got to stop living in fear."

"I'm fine! I'm driving the freeway!"

"That's wonderful, hon'."

It is tempting to place blame on Rosie for "prescribing" our mother's move back to her native California. Born and raised in Ventura, Margaret became a "camp follower" trailing the lives of her daughters after her divorce. She lived vicariously through Rosie whom she followed the most, living up the street from her at numerous addresses, even during my sister's medical residency in Boston, then near Rosie's home in Ann Arbor until finally moving to Venice and the other side of the alley from me. Now it is my turn to have our mother close by, and I perceive my dreaded future: Margaret and me, forever codependent and squabbling like the mother-daughter duo in their decrepit old mansion in that movie, "Gray Gardens."

And yet, Mother has been a friend and confidant during the worst of these past two years when profound sorrow gave way to anxiety, dizzy spells, debilitating migraines. She filled the Imitrex prescriptions, stocked my medicine cabinet with Advil, brewed strong coffee and poured colas. She was a true comfort when even a trip to the grocery store was an expedition worthy of Lewis and Clark. But as I begin to emerge from my chrysalis of mourning she remains watchful and hovering, eager to be "Mommy" still. Which is why, standing at my front door in t-shirt and jeans, sipping fresh-brewed coffee, I hear my neighbor's Dalmatians' calamitous barks turning to happy whines and see my mother's delicate hand, recognizable with its ubiquitous amethyst gemstone from Brasilia, reaching over the picket fence to pet their squirmy heads.

Margaret adores dogs, has an innate ability to recognize the good from the homicidal, and talks to them in a chirpy, dog-conversational voice, the one she's using now. She then unlocks and opens my gate, slips the key back into her puffy imitation Chanel bag, and trudges up the walkway.

She is tiny and formidable. Her white hair is cut short and spikey and she wears all black — black slacks, turtleneck, Converse high-tops. A purple glass beaded necklace and her amethyst ring are the only spots of color in this ensemble. She ignores the explosion of orange poppies in my garden and rather stares intently at me as she approaches, her face drawn by concern. It's the face looming over me in childhood checking to see if I have a fever.

"Is that coffee?" she asks in a noticeably different tone than the one she used on the dogs, "Do you have a headache?"

"Mocha Java. And no, I don't have a headache."

I turn back into the house. Mother follows me with quick determined steps, her attention so fixated on me I can hear her inhaling.

"You seem, I don't know, nervous," she says. At seven-thirty in the morning, she looks like a saleswoman in an expensive dress shop, her sharp features flawlessly made up with Christian Dior products. Once a dynamo, fashionable beauty, and surprising trooper in her day, Margaret efficiently packed our household whenever we transferred to a new country. There were revolutions, anti-American riots and kidnappings, yet during those times she rose to the occasion while sending the mixed messages that would unfailingly confound us. When Rosie and I were out at night in Cali with friends, for instance, she didn't think about how her teenage daughters were living in a country where revolutionaries cut the throats of businessmen and made *corbatas* out of their tongues. Instead she fretted about teenage pregnancy or if a cough meant tuberculosis or a rash from a spider bite would spread into a full-blown poisonous, incurable infection. Bodyguards would accompany us on school buses to our high school in the Colombian countryside, but she was more concerned about us swimming near the country club pool drain and it sucking out our intestines than of armed assassins prowling the streets on motorcycles.

Divorce and her overseas adventures decades behind, Mother has shown up for work today, and her job is me.

"I saw Winston on the roof again," she says, "One of these days he's going to slide off and those dogs will tear him limb from limb. If he doesn't die from the fall."

"Well, I can't supervise the cats full time," I say, although I am worried. I don't want Winston's blood on my hands. I love Winston.

I reach for my water bottle in case I have a hot flash and slip some Advil in my jeans pocket in case I get *one of those* headaches. I tuck into my bag more Tums and Kleenex and my phone and some energy bars and a banana since I'm going to be gone from the house at least two hours. I put on my chrysoprase crystal talisman necklace which I sort-of think, but not really, but hope will protect me from harm. In my head is an image I swear Mother has telepathically transferred to me: My pick-up truck slipping from my control and sliding across freeway lanes and over the divider into an oncoming semi. This image grabs hold and stays as I wash and dry my coffee mug and then scrub the sink. Like Rosie, I keep a very clean house.

"Dalmatians can be vicious," Margaret persists, "I heard a story —"

"Don't tell me right now."

"I think you'll want to hear this —"

"No, I don't. And please don't give the cats any Xanax, okay?"

Margaret has been known to spike the cats' food with her medication, having concluded my cats and hers are highly nervous creatures in need of sedation. Mother really looks distraught and I'm about to suggest that she take one herself, but if this happens she'll only spread the joy and I want my cats drug free.

"Come on, Mother, I've got to go. Winston will be fine, really. Let's hope."

I grab my keys, and since Margaret doesn't take the hint that it's time for her to go too, I do what I usually do, which is let her stick around and supervise the cats and check the stove and hair dryer and iron and coffee machine and microwave half a dozen times to see that they're off before leaving and locking my door with the duplicate key I never should have given her.

"No Xanax!" I shout over my shoulder as she stands on the front stoop with a look of stoicism, like I'm setting sail over the edge of the world.

I approach my Ford Ranger parked on the street and see my neighbors in their modern fishbowl house feeding their baby. They wave as I walk past, and as I return the gesture I wonder if I'll be back this afternoon or if they will be discussing my demise over cocktails this evening.

A giant Westinghouse, they'll say, *she never knew what hit her.*

"You're most vulnerable in a familiar environment."

Magill Landscaping, in an area of Venice known as the "Oakwood Triangle," is set within an eclectic garden of dramatic iron sculptures and aloes. A few blocks away is Abbot Kinney Boulevard where former artists lofts have been replaced by three star restaurants and designer shops with t-shirts that say, "Venice: Where Art Meets Crime." During the Rodney King riots neighbors raced over to Magill's to put out a fire in his front room, the only damage being melted Venetian blinds and some landscape drawings. The culprits turned out to be local kids who'd gone to the after school programs at the nearby Neighborhood Youth Association Children's Center financed by the VGHT, or Venice Gardens and Homes Tour, ironically founded by Magill. The kids later apologized, and though rioting continued to blaze in other parts of the city, Magill went on with business in his exuberantly cool-headed way by paying the kids to work a few hours planting vegetables at the Children's Center.

This is my community, where we leant a hand to one another after the Northridge Earthquake, where we stood together on the beach watching the fires creep down the Palisades hillsides and where we meet for

Neighborhood Watch updates and send notices on our local blog about missing pets or stolen laptops. On the days I walk to Magill's Landscaping I know that the big man with the lead pipe slung across his shoulder is a sweetheart named Joe, that the tattooed teens skateboarding by were once the infants whose diapers I'd changed, that the disheveled woman who screams like a banshee from her front porch swing is finishing her dissertation on Yeats.

Raul, Enrique, Gabriella and Marcello arrive from the nursery in the landscaping truck with twenty-four inch boxes of palms, giant Birds of Paradise and wisteria. Magill comes out of his office piqued and disgruntled because his clients have requested a tropical landscape despite his repeated warnings they should use fire-retardant plants.

"They live in a fire zone," Magill grumbles. In his sixties, ruggedly sinewy and temperamental, he's comfortably shabby-looking with a mussed white afro and slouchy jeans.

"You," Magill says to me as, cactus mix up to my elbows, I complete the finishing touches on my planters, "What're you doing, they're perfect, leave them alone. Jorge, get these into her pickup."

Jorge and Raul lift the seven large glazed pots into the back of my truck. They're filled with drought tolerant "thrillers, fillers and spillers" of pale yellow and green striped aloe, feathery *euphorbia* with tiny white blooms, and groupings of purple and pale green succulents cascading down over the sides. I adjust the succulents and fluff the *euphorbia* blooms as they go in.

"Que piensas?" I ask Jorge.

"Es bueno," Jorge reassures me, nodding. I climb up into the back of my pickup and join Raul in tucking the plants carefully under protective plastic. I don't want the wind turning them into the garden equivalent of a Phyllis Diller hairdo.

"Someone tried to break into Violet's," Magill says in reference to the early morning police helicopter activity. He gestures to the paint-chipped old Craftsman across the street with the swing on its porch. Violet is the banshee working on her Yeats dissertation. Pity the poor robber who goes after her.

"Is she okay?"

"Is *he* okay's more like it," Magill says, "Violet slammed the intruder in the back of the head with a crowbar then called the police. The guy's going to have one hell of a concussion if not brain damage."

"Who was he?"

"Ex-boyfriend," Magill shrugs, "I suggest you don't mention this to your mother or I won't hear the end of it."

"What, am I crazy? Don't answer that."

Born of a Haitian mother and Hollywood set designer and raised in all parts of multiracial Los Angeles, Magill cannot abide Mother's paranoid suburban mom act.

"Know where you're going?"

"Newport Beach, I have the address."

Magill slits his blue eyes at me in mock scrutiny. He knows this is a big thing for me, how I've struggled to control the panic attacks that, as he puts it, "keep you from being the thee you want to be."

"You're going to love this Newport landscape," he says, "It was written up in *International Gardens* last fall and designed by an up and coming Colombian landscape artist for what's rumored to be some cartel muckety-muck."

I slip behind the wheel and hope my pickup has the horsepower to get this heavy load to Orange County. I don't hear "cartel," I don't even hear "muckety-muck." Because what Magill really is saying is that by driving out of my little three-mile radius comfort zone and daring to reinstate the beauty of native plants into the seemingly soulless overdeveloped and sprawling cityscape that is Southern California, I'm participating in an environmental "back to the garden" revolution. I'm a part of something again, something that matters, and he's right as only Magill can be. And so with my pickup of sustainable planters, I'm back in the game. *Viva la revolucion.*

— —

"Don't stand under power lines.
One could come loose, swoop down and
electrocute you."

My truck engine revs high, burdened by the heavy load. Vehicles speed past. I press my foot to the accelerator and soon I've joined the pack on the 405 — the woman in the Saturn talking into a headset; the Humvee blasting music so loud I can feel the bass rocking the asphalt; the helmeted man in a business suit on the Harley. I push it up to 65 mph. My head is hot. I blast the air-conditioning into my face. I turn on the radio. Innocuous L.A.-appropriate Santana accompanies the jets screaming toward LAX. Liquid crystal billboards and brassy balloons float over shiny car dealerships sporting ads for SUVs.

I'm flying, flying on the freeway on a Friday morning...

...and now I'm slowing, slowing to a crawl. I laugh, almost deliriously relieved. What was I so afraid of? It's rush hour and we're moving at twenty miles per hour. Now slower. Now stopping. It's a parking lot.

I switch to AC Music — After Charlie — because music from the time of Charlie, which covers some five years of my life, can crash and burn my heart. Salsa from the Afro-Cuban band Sono-Lux is okay and so is the Latin reggae rockers Mandorico, as none of that music is infused with the places Charlie and I had been, not his apartment in Burbank, or our cross-country drives in his old '72 Mustang.

I met Charlie on the set of a bad film called *High Octane*. He was past fifty and, but for his lined, sun-darkened face, had the body of a man twenty years younger. As a stuntman Charlie performed death-defying feats like jumping from ten story windows and crashing motorcycles into trucks and dodging speeding Hummers. He was not one to dwell on fear — how could he? He told me the trick to doing a good stunt was being prepared and following all safety rules. He also recognized in me his opposite -- a self-insulated woman if not for his bright and daring intrusion into my life. This is not to say that I hadn't had lovers, just none that stuck around. There had been "The Director" while I was in film school, "The Writer" as I labored over several unexceptional screenplays. There was "The Married One" and a number of others after: "The Carpenter," "The Musician," "The Backpacker." There was no blaming anyone but myself for our liaisons failing to last, because with every one I kept secret my long history of anxiety and panic. I would claim I was having "a little insomnia" when I'd rise in the middle of the night, heart racing; I would sneak Xanax before airplane flights or if that wasn't available, simply drink a lot. There were interrogations and accusations, and I came to realize that as far as relationships were concerned, I preferred the courtship and pursuit more than settling down. Then I bought my little house in Venice — just in time for Charlie to move in and be my head contractor, both figuratively and literally.

Charlie never became "The Stuntman," but rather instead "The One."

Then one night while filming in Lancaster he just happened to be standing in the wrong place. An electrical wire formerly attributed to Mother's inflamed imagination fetched loose, swooped down, and obliterated the human being who was Charlie. It is one of life's little absurdities that Charlie was killed not during a dangerous stunt but in a situation as random as that wire coming loose in a Santa Ana wind. The wire touched Charlie and he was gone in half a second, electrocuted out of his life. In one half a second everything I had assimilated in our time together — how to board an airplane without fear, how to eat strange new foods, how to sit in the passenger seat of a Ferrari going a hundred — went right out the window. And in his place Mother moved in.

And so. Driving to Newport, I forgo Clapton and the blues and Booker T. and any other music that would conjure Charlie. Instead I listen to the steady salsa rhythms that send me back to early childhood in Guatemala and eerie recollections of another kind. Rosie is two; I am five. It is Sunday. Our parents sleep off party hangovers while we help ourselves to the dregs of crème de menthe and Kahlua left in the bottom of cocktail glasses in the living room. Live-in housekeepers Chita and Lili give us bites from their tamale pie and take us to the downtown religious parade. We learn to genuflect when Mother Mary swathed in flowers and written prayers floats by and a funereal drumbeat announces the star of the show: Giant Jesus the Bogeyman, a sort-of saintly Freddy Krueger nailed to the cross, eyes raised in agony, painted blood running down from the crown of thorns on his plaster-of-Paris brow. He's coming to get me, the child who never did buy into the Sunday school tales about Jesus loving all the children. My crème de menthe breakfast turns the parade crowd lurid. I may be five, but I know that evil is all around in the streets of Guatemala City. The trampled carnations, that crown of thorns, the desperate prayers of His worshippers and the bloodied Jesus himself are confirmation that all is not well in the world and one better beware.

— ~

"Remember to call me when you get there. For all I know, you could be lying in a ditch somewhere."

The house for the wedding reception is a stunner, if you like this sort of thing. It looks like Tara: Columns, a sweep of perpetually thirsty green lawn, wisteria dripping from a sun porch, everything but the peacocks and antebellum gowns. I understand now why the wedding event planner responded so enthusiastically to my decorative planters featured in January's issue of *Garden Design*. With their clouds of white blooming *euphorbia* and lavender *echeveria*, they will serve as sentries leading up the brick walkway to the party tent billowing in the soft morning breeze. I jump down from my truck and search for someone to unload my creations but all I see is a group of nervous ladies talking in Spanish to a flower deliveryman carrying a massive arrangement.

As the ladies appear preoccupied with their singular task, I wander across the lawn and beyond the long infinity pool toward another area of the property. There is definitely big money here, but unlike the massive columnar house and its thirsty lawn, this back sweep of landscaping is easy and elegant, as if some unseen landscaper's hand had refined nature. Olive trees and lavender form a gentle wave curving along the hillside and down toward the sea. The olives' beautifully gnarled trunks and thin silvery leaves shimmer on branches expertly and artfully pruned into a filigree frame before the Pacific Ocean beyond. It is breathtaking. I wonder who the landscaper is and who the clients are, identified on the down payment checks simply as "Corrida Inc."

More Spanish speaking voices and steady clip-clip sounds draw me down the slope where a crew is being supervised by a lean man with thick peppery dark hair who expertly wields pruning shears, working a low hanging branch in demonstration. From my distance I can see the man appears instructive, reverent in his task, while by contrast in the uppermost branches of another tree a chattering, distracted teenager cuts with an electric chainsaw. It's the perfect set-up for some slasher pic, and just as I'm thinking of how the disaster might unfold, the supervisor shouts a warning at the very instant the boy loses his footing and falls, the waist support suspending him and the chainsaw slipping from his grasp. Workers leap out of the way, avoiding chopped limbs and decapitated heads, and the saw rips into the ground, jumping and vibrating until someone shuts it off.

The boss man springs up onto a lower branch and climbs swiftly. He's wearing what appears to be finely tailored linen pants, too nice for tree climbing, but his body moves with agility and he grabs the rope and begins pulling the boy up until he pauses suddenly and lets him dangle. The workers shout up advice but the boss man orders *"silencio."* I catch the drift of his Spanish as he scolds the youth for risking the safety of others, and not until the kid whines a frightened apology does the boss man quietly haul him up, face dark with exertion. With the boy safely on the branch he gently cuffs his head, all smiles now, joking even. The kid humbly thanks him and the workers break into *"bravos"* of applause.

Graceful as a big cat, the man climbs back to the ground, brushes olive leaves from those soft linen pants, and instructs his workers to resume. The message is clear: Don't cross this man.

Having paused to observe this incredible scene, I only now continue down the slope toward this alpha-male-in-charge. He briefly glances at me, looks back toward his workers, then turns to observe me yet again, this time more closely.

Mildly, perhaps more than mildly curious, he scrutinizes me walking toward him, and I recall what it signifies, how it feels. Attraction, whether human or animal, is abruptly powerful and empowering. Unencumbered by purse or skirt, I swing my arms, my loose jeans and t-shirt all but saying, "I dress for comfort, not men like you." He seems to register this challenge with a faint smile.

One of the workers is saying *Senior de la Torre*, and it is the combination of the spoken name and the sudden visual shock of recognition that enables me to comprehend suddenly what I couldn't register or believe. I know this man. Or rather, the boy he was. Yes, I know him. And as I get closer, he arrives at the same conclusion.

"Mira," he says in a voice as low and mellifluous as the honeyed scent of frangipani on a tropical breeze.

"Alejandro de la Torre," I say, then add, "I presume," as if I were Stanley encountering Livingstone in the deepest jungles of the Congo.

He was the one who ignited the earliest flush of desire in me. When we were young in Cali, Columbia. The year he was kidnapped by the FARC.

"You are the same!" Alejandro says, "I would know you anywhere," and I believe him. I say, "You too" and mean it. I see the boy I knew in the face of the man that is no longer soft. The edges of his eyes are etched and his jaw hardened and rough with stubble and the prettiness is gone and yet I see the dark-eyed son of my father's boss, Ignacio de la Torre, president of a division of Uniroyal International in Columbia. I see him arriving in a formal suit to take me to a dinner dance at *Club Campestre* and I see how he looked two months later after he returned from the jungle.

He was sent away to a private school in Switzerland after that and I never saw him again.

"Mira Mira Mira," he says softly, touching my face in his palms, and I know that what he means is "look." His workers half watch us. There is no hesitation when he pulls me into him, and I feel the intake of his breathing and hug back, as if by holding him tightly we can erase time separating our last embrace in a river in the jungle in a place called San Cipriano, before the kidnapping, when he brought me to the cusp of the person I might have become.

"Your mother took you and your sister back to California," he says.

"And you were sent to school in Switzerland."

"Your father remained in Cali."

"Until he was transferred to the Uniroyal office in New York."

"Our letters just stopped."

"You stopped writing."

"No, it was you."

"Was it?"

I don't dispute it but it was he who had stopped. And why not? He was older by a year and much had happened to him.

"My father never fully recovered," he says. I remember that his father had been shot by *las Fuerzas* when he was kidnapped. "But he is now at peace. My parents are both deceased."

"My father too."

"I am sorry."

"So am I."

'Sorry' for me means all of it — how I was unable to grow up fast enough. My final letters had been appeals from a naïve American girl and even as I was writing them I knew that who I had been to him and who I could be had ended. It was a terrifying time for the de la Torres and many families. All of it — our family together, Alejandro and I — it all ended even before I knew it was ending.

"And your mother," he says, "Is she well?"

"Mom is fine. She lives near me now."

"A charming woman. Always more fun than the other mothers."

More fun indeed! When Alejandro picked me up for a date, Father would invite him in for a beer and Mother would engage the handsome young man in conversation, speaking animatedly to him about our English class assignment on "Lord of the Flies." Later, after Alejandro was being held by *las Fuerzas*, she would wonder aloud if he was "going native" among his captors in the jungle or if, like Piggy, he would be killed by child savages.

"Yes, Mom's a fun one," I say.

"How do you know of Mauricio Corrida?"

His question about our client is abruptly unexpected.

"I don't know him at all. Magill got this gig. I'm a designer with his landscaping firm. Jake Magill."

"So you are the designer of these famous planters! I am so very happy to see your lovely face again, dear Mira!"

He signals another worker to take over and guides me back up the slope of lawn toward the house, arm around my waist. Adjusting my comfort level, I recall the boy who read my journal and carried me through the olive grove along *Rio Cali* when my feet were blistered from dancing *la cumbia*. Our brief time together was overshadowed by a revolution that has lasted decades and which, despite the current peace talks, has kept his country under siege by corruption, American interference, drug wars and kidnappings, yet letting go of that time was one of the hardest things I'd ever done in my young life.

Now the man, no longer a boy, muses aloud over the likelihood of me walking into his life on a hillside mansion in Newport Beach, California, of all places. He tells me he's designed this landscape for his friend, Mauricio Corrida, and at the reception tent he introduces me to Mauricio's lovely fiancée Isabella, an excitable young woman who refers to me as the "miraculous lady of the urns" whose planter designs have become the "*horticultural objects de jour.*"

"You landscape is beautiful," I say, pulling my gaze away from the impossible immediate proximity of Alejandro's profile and resting my sights on the sweeping, dazzling view. I wonder if he is married.

"I assist Nature display her natural beauty," he says.

"You are falsely modest, Alejandro."

"You know me too well, Mira."

We gaze together across the infinity pool and the olive trees framing the ocean beyond, and as we stand together it's as if the last forty years haven't happened and I'm still the girl wearing the hat my father gave me which said "The World Is My Oyster."

"When you let down your guard is when you need to worry."

M id-morning passes in a soft, luminescent blur. It's a Truffaut film, sunlight suffusing every judiciously chosen shot. There is the wedding party preparing for tomorrow's event, the beautiful bride and the anticipated arrival of her distinguished groom, there is the elegant luncheon set on the terrace, and finally we have Alejandro directing his crew to situate my planters onto the walkway leading up to the wedding tent, turning them to be viewed at their best angles while casually dropping the plants' Latin nomenclature.

Introductions to the luncheon party include not only the Spanish bride Isabella but two exquisitely coifed older women who are the absent groom's sisters and a young man who appears to be their shopping escort or secretary. I am invited to join them on the terrace for seafood salads, where we overlook a glimmering distant sea. Alejandro speaks with easy confidence and when he translates the Spanish conversation I don't remind him I have some rudimentary knowledge of the language, so taken am I by his gallant attention toward putting me at ease. Even at sixteen he was a sophisticated jetsetter, returning to his mother's native Switzerland, passing through Paris and absorbing its influence. Now I recall I've seen "Torre Landscapes" in architectural design magazines, never realizing the artfully arranged tropical and Mediterranean plantings were the work of the boy who once laid atop me on a couch whispering *mi niña bonita*.

Conversation is an international cornucopia of Spanish, Italian, English and French, and with reluctance I refuse the proffered champagne everyone is drinking. I don't ask where the groom is or what his business is or how he happens to have acquired a house in Newport Beach among apparently other global residences. Instead I listen to Alejandro conversationally skip from Spanish to Italian and back to English, all the while disbelieving that this immense world would have shrunk enough to bring us back together.

Suddenly my cellphone rings a jarring wake-up call, a jolt ripping into the languid afternoon. My hosts turn with expressions of concern. I quickly apologize and answer, stopping the loud old-fashioned ring. I've forgotten to call Mother.

"Are you alright? Are you okay?"

My breath drops into my diaphragm and the old anxiety floods over me in a flash. As if on cue, the sun pops behind the one small cloud in the sky and the Truffaut frolic turns Hitchcockian. I stand up and walk away from the table.

"I'm fine," I say. I don't tell her about Alejandro because I want this moment for myself, if simply for the afternoon. "I'm having lunch here."

"You said you'd call when you arrived. I thought you'd driven into a ditch."

"I don't recall seeing any ditches on the 405, Mother."

"You know what I mean."

She reminds me the cats need to be fed, that I'd promised her I'd be home in a few hours and that promised arrival time has already passed. I'm late, late for a date with my cats and Mother, and suddenly I feel one of my headaches coming on. I think about taking a couple Advil on the drive home even though the plastic water bottle in my truck has been baking in the sun and could give me cancer. Cancer later or headache now, I decide on cancer later and dig into my jeans pocket for the two pills I put there this morning just-in-case. Alejandro has left the table and is now standing by my side. I disconnect Mother's mid-stream warning about a sig alert on the Garden Grove, and when I say I have to go he gives a disappointed sigh that is quaintly feminine, his down-turned smile mocking his own sentimentality.

"You cannot disappear from my life again," he says. I agree, but for me it is more than a nicety or polite conversation. In the back of my mind I see it, feel it, how it had been when I was fifteen, with him, with all of life and the world ahead of us, and I wonder: If I was to go back to that time and start over, would I have grown up to be bolder and more adventuresome? Would I be doing something else with my life now other than having dinner with my mother and hurrying home to feed the cats?

I thank the hosts, say my goodbyes, and collect the check for my services from Mauricio's assistant, Arnoldo, a brooding fellow who appears unhappy about everything and everyone having a good time. Bride-to-be Isabella gives me a girlish wave and I think of how incredibly nice everyone is and how I'd rather stay for champagne.

"Was that a husband who called?" Alejandro asks when he escorts me back to my truck.

"Oh, yes, one of many," I laugh, then add, "No, no husband."

"Children?"

"No," I say, "But lots of cats." I instantly regret this admission. What man wants to hear a woman is a cat lady?

"Ah, so this is how you have kept your teenage body."

I catch his open appraisal of my blue-jeaned hips as I step up into the Ranger and find it refreshing, fun to be acknowledged as a woman.

"Yeah, I guess, although children would have been great."

"Boyfriend?"

He shuts the door and leans toward me, his hand on the roof of the truck, eyes laughing with self-deprecating bemusement at his own need to know.

"No boyfriend," I answer. "And you?"

Something goes blank behind his eyes and I think, yes, a wife, but then turning back on the lightness and charm he says, "No." I instantly figure he's lying, and to cover my awareness of why he would lie, I talk about the upcoming garden tour and how I must return to Venice and Magill and our tight schedule and even more pressing commitments.

Gotta run, I'm saying, away from you.

"Your work is admirable," he says, undaunted, "and I thank-you on behalf of Mauricio and Isabella. And now I would like to see you again, if I may call?"

I fumble in the glove compartment for my business cards and hand him one, and I'm back in the Truffaut film just for a moment before I think, *no, make this just business,* landscaping business rather than unfinished business.

He slips the card into the front pocket of his cotton shirt with the rolled up sleeves and when he gives me the traditional kiss on one cheek then the other I try to resist feeling the heat of his bristled skin and fail.

He has observed and seen me, and only now am I aware that I have not been seen, actually looked at by a man, in some time. And yet, we have changed; every part of our bodies and minds has been altered by our separate histories. *In all sensibility* I lecture myself, *be sensible.* After all, what does he want from me? I'm too old for him; I'm his age, after all. This is not an absurd thought, the idea of being too old for a man my own age. And so, as a *businesswoman,* the *garden designer,* I invite him to join *us* at Magill Landscaping's Venice Garden and Home Tour kick-off party at Magill's house in the Palisades, and he breaks into a winning smile and promises to be there.

As I pull away I wash down the two Advils with the warm carcinogenic Arrowhead water and warn myself to pay attention, as I will be heading home west into the headache-inducing glare of sunset.

I drive down the long winding roadway leading away from Tara loo-kalike and glance in my rear view mirror at Alejandro waving good-bye. I wonder if he will come to Magill's or if the past is irreparable and this will truly be the last time I see him. And as I'm watching his mirrored image I see his wave suddenly stop in mid-air, and turning my gaze back to the road I encounter a motorcade of at least six Mercedes SUVs, all shiny black, entering the gateway to the estate, winding their way up the long drive.

The driver of the first car appears positively funereal in his dark sunglasses. Subsequent riders in the front seats, each with identical sunglasses, barely glance my way and tinted windows obscure any view I might have of whoever may be seated in back. *Damn Magill*, I think, for planting the seed of suspicion in my mind.

There's no denying it; *these guys are heavies.*

"Some house cleaning products mixed together emit lethal fumes.
I just can't remember which ones."

When I arrive home Margaret is predictably sitting on my front porch with Winston in her lap. She's drinking an it's-going-to-be-a-bumpy-night martini and her freshly lip-sticked mouth is set in a straight hot-pink line.

"Hi," I say, as I approach with my keys, although I don't need my keys since my front door is wide open. She has apparently spent the whole day at her "office," i.e. my home.

"You look tired," she says. Her tone is one of remonstration.

"I am."

"I bet the drive was just terrible."

"It wasn't bad," I say, "How are things here? Are the cats okay? Did they survive without Xanax?"

Best defense, good offense, and Margaret's lips give a little twitch, indicating that someone, somewhere, had Xanax today and she won't be sharing who. That leaves two of us with secrets. The languid afternoon with Alejandro seems centuries away, and while I intend to tell Margaret about it sooner or later, I want to protect it for the time being from her tainted view even though I feel stingy withholding the information, as she adored Alejandro.

"Why don't you come over and I'll cook us dinner," Margaret says, "We can watch that movie."

She's been talking for days about a movie she's already watched several times about a mother in Wisconsin who goes on a rampage and stabs her husband and children to death in their sleep. What makes it particularly fascinating to her is that it's based on a true story.

"Not tonight, Mom, I'm really beat, as you can imagine. But thanks for the invitation."

Usually she argues until I break down and agree to come over, but she senses something different this time.

"Are you all right?"

I've heard this question probably ten thousand times in my life, and never once have I felt that she's really asking, but rather telling me I'm *not* alright.

"I'm fine, thank-you. Feel free to finish your drink before you go."

My abrupt formality seems to put her off for a minute, but I'm not interested in gauging her response. I head to the refrigerator and pull out a Coke.

"Headache?"

"A little. I just need a little peace and quiet and I'll be fine."

I guzzle half the Coke down and start sweeping up the bits of wax paper and cracker crumbs Mother has deposited, like some mad mouse on a raid, across the counter and kitchen floor.

"Something happened today," she says.

"Well, yes, I guess you could say that," I reply, remembering Alejandro's face. "And I promise I will tell you all about it later. Deal?"

Stand off acknowledged, she replies, "Deal," but as she leaves, she issues a parting shot:

"Don't forget while you're busy with your housework that you're not supposed to combine certain cleaners. I don't want to come back here and find you unconscious on the kitchen floor!"

"Ha ha," I say, because she's joking. Sort of. Not really.

⌐ ⌐

I fling off my soiled t-shirt and jeans and step into the claw foot tub in the garden shed at the back of the house beside glazed pots with orchids and bromeliads in varying stages of bloom. *Perhaps there is life after Charlie*. The thought seems almost blasphemous. God could strike me down and drown me in three inches of bathwater for even daring to consider it.

Alejandro was the magical boy, the one with the dark chocolate curls and the brows like blackbird wings in flight. From the moment I laid eyes on him at the Cali Hotel bar when Father first introduced us to his boss and family, I was catapulted into that sweet haze of first desire. Our pairing was an unlikely prospect — me, the girl in the pink dress sucking her Shirley Temple through a straw, and he, the worldly young scion with a Cuba Libre, politely claiming Castro's revolution was deserving respect.

His heroes were Che and Neruda, and when he spoke in history class even the inattentive listened. Mother said he would be president of Colombia someday but I thought no, he was not that kind of ambitious, for he admired beauty too much — the beauty of gardens, poetry, girls, movies. When I joined the track team and rode on the bus to the inter-school competitions in Medellin, I snuck peeks at Alejandro playing soccer with other students, rebels, and young cocaine smugglers — I didn't care or know the difference. He would say, "Mira, Mira," as if to say, "Look, Mira, look outward," and I did. I joined his community project at the local orphanage; we painted classrooms and read stories to children until Mother, convinced I would contract cholera if not lice, ordered me home on weekends. I aspired to be a woman with him while simultaneously mired in child-hood and Mother's persistent dominion, but we found secret places near the polo field at *Club Campestre* and fields beyond, in the tropical meadows behind *Colegio Bolivar* where sudden warm thundershowers and brilliant rainbows were commonplace. It seemed we were always warm and wet, kissing in rain, kissing in whirlpools.

And then, almost as if a vengeful God were punishing us for our pleasure, he was kidnapped. I was home studying when it happened, un-aware of how in that very moment he was being taken, unaware until hours later Mother came into my room, sat on the bed and told me. The kidnapping occurred following an after-school soccer match. His father had come to the match in the family limousine and had been shot in the stomach; Alejandro was grabbed by two men and driven away in a black van.

A month passed, then another. Ignacio de la Torre nearly died of his wounds but recovered enough to receive the ransom demands sent by *las Fuerzas*. There was some debate as to whether the ransom was either mysteriously acquired or Alejandro escaped, but in either case he returned from his incarceration, no longer my boyfriend, and no longer a boy.

He came to our house accompanied by his parents. His father wasted thin from the gunshot wound, his elegant Swiss mother quietly tense. They drank tea with my parents in the living room while his bodyguard stood outside my bedroom. He told me he was going away to school in Switzerland then shook my hand in a formal manner. I wanted more and kissed him, and when he didn't kiss back I reminded him of how we'd run away to San Cipriano and what we had done. He made no reply but rather held me back and looked at me with a distant fondness as if I were a treat he once enjoyed but now found too sweet for his liking. And then he was gone.

Decades have passed since that time, and yet the ghost of the teenage girl I had been shadows me now as I step out of the bath and dry off and pull on clean jeans and t-shirt. I was a nervous teenager who drank too much Coca-Cola and pined for boys who could soothe my anxiety, yet no one made a connection between my caffeine consumption and sleepless nights. The household was preoccupied with other concerns, such as the beginning of the end or our parents' marriage. Plus I'd set my sights on leaving home for college in the States where, away from parental tensions, I would eventually learn the benefits of cognitive thinking.

And yet, a mystery remains from that time in Colombia, an elusive something I can barely put my finger on. Perhaps this is why I must see Alejandro again, and why, as I go about the rest of my evening, heating soup, watering the garden and feeding the cats, I wonder who the grown-up man is that the boy Alejandro became.

"Don't eat anything with mushrooms at a party or restaurant. They could turn out to be toadstools and poison you."

— —

Mother is fidgety on the drive to Magill's party, and I attribute this to a variety of reasons. She doesn't get out much, and despite being impeccably dressed in a striking pale yellow Ralph Lauren jacket and flowery silk skirt, her thick short hair spiked and white, she's insecure about socializing. Plus it means having to eat food she herself hasn't prepared, which is invariably suspect.

Margaret is also worked-up about meeting Alejandro, whom I've said will be at Magill's. When I finally told her about our amazing coincidental meeting in Newport Beach, she was astounded for about half a second before wanting to know the sensationalist details about the kidnapping that occurred decades ago.

"Do you think he was tortured?" she asks out of the blue as I'm driving up Chautaugua. "It must have been terrible to see his father shot like that, and shot in the stomach too. I hear stomach wounds are particularly bloody and gruesome."

She ruminates on the blood and gore as we continue our drive up into the lovely hills of Pacific Palisades, not seeing the massive trees, palatial homes and glorious gardens bursting into bloom.

"You know, Mother," I say, "For Alejandro that might not be the best topic of conversation tonight."

"Nonsense. It was the most important event in his life. He probably can't forget it if he wanted to. It's something I wouldn't ever be able to forget, being kidnapped like that. I wonder if he was raped. *Sodomized*."

"Why don't you ask him?"

"I would never ask a man something like that," she says, failing to pick up on my sarcasm, and now she's truly agitated.

"Of course you wouldn't," I say, "You are the model of conversational restraint."

She glances over to see if I'm pulling her leg and when she realizes I am she huffs out a nervous little bark of rare self-deprecating humor. As confounded as I am by her fascination with all things monstrous and tragic and macabre, you can say this for her, she's never boring. Plus sometimes Margaret has a way of surprising. Just when you think she's going to be impossible, she rallies and shines. I hope that will be the case tonight and I won't have to drive her home in a funk because no one was interested in discussing the details of Princess Diana's death in the tunnel.

I turn Margaret's Volvo over to the valet and we join the other arriving guests. There are up-and-comers and also a few celebrities; young artists, actors and business people who want to make a difference by donating their homes to the Tour charity drive but who also want to be seen in their Bruno Magli loafers and Pucci jackets. Mother isn't gawking at anyone however as we climb the stairs to Magill's impressive entryway flanked by two of my terra cotta planters. Margaret doesn't notice these either. Suddenly she grabs my elbow.

"Remember," she says, "Don't eat —"

"— anything with mushrooms. Got it."

Magill leaves a group of guests to glide over to us. He is in top mode: grandly talkative and insouciantly attired in slouchy jeans and a loose Afghan Kuchi shirt, his Afro gleaming silver.

"Come, Margaret," he says, wrapping Mother's arm in his, "Come see my portrait of Lauren of the Greatest Generation, of which you are one."

He is referring to his giant black and white picture of Lauren Bacall behind his baby grand and she responds with exclamations of polite interest I hope she can sustain.

"He's out there," Magill says to me with a quick over-his-shoulder aside that I register to mean my Colombian guest.

Out on the patio, Venice's Councilman is talking sustainable gardens and thanking the big donors and homeowners for opening both their homes and wallets on behalf of the Neighborhood Youth Association's Children's Center. I wave hello to some clients then step across the patio and past the swimming pool with its floating ornamental balls to the large expanse of back garden that is classic Magill: Playful, beautiful, innovative.

Sweeping pathways of crushed rock edge drought-tolerant grasses and eucalyptus trees bend finger leaves down over the hillside, their tangy, faintly medicinal scent lingering in the air. Fire pits blaze in jewel-toned alcoves with built-in seating and people congregate around the fires to warm themselves from the brief nip of chill in the air. The sun dips onto the band of ocean horizon, and it is from my position at the back of this landscape, looking out toward the sunset, that I see Alejandro's silhouette moving toward me, his clothing draped carelessly yet elegantly on his frame. I am wearing long white silk pants and a wrap-around tunic in homage to Old Hollywood. He pauses in his approach, and by this he demonstrates that he is taking me in. The graciousness of this gesture is in itself seductive.

"You are a vision," says he and, taking my hands, kisses me in the European manner on each cheek. A few people in our vicinity turn to observe us. Alejandro certainly is watchable. Everything about him

warrants attention — his precise Castilian accent, his fluidity of movement. I think of Sade's song *Smooth Operator*.

"You've met Magill?" I ask.

"I have. And the Councilman. And these —" He points to the firepits
and lounge areas, "— Spectacular."

We pause at the farthest most firepit and as I describe Magill's design
process, I experience the impression of stepping in and out of the moment: When I am "in" I am merely conversing with an old friend and
landscape designer with whom I share the commonality of past and an
interest in garden design. When I am "out" I am made aware of his un-
avoidable sexuality, the alpha male in polite society possibly capable of
seducing me by simply standing here and looking. At me.

"This is *exquisito*," he says, gesturing to but not quite touching the
blue green crystal hanging on its chain between my breasts.

"Chrysoprase," I say, "The gemstone is — it has all kinds of so-called
healing properties."

At the risk of sounding New Agey I run down the list — the crystal
helps clarify problems, calm anxiety, draw out the unconscious mind to
the conscious. It strengthens insight.

"And it encourages hope and joy," I add, feeling truly ridiculous.
Having run out of words I reach inside my overheated brain matter for an
opinion, observation, something, but come up empty handed.

"You were always a joyous person," he says, and then I feel the barely discernible touch of his fingertips moving lightly down between my
shoulder blades. I step back, a movement that says *not so fast*. He responds
with a surprised look. *Maybe old girlfriends aren't so easy after all.*

"I must ask you something," I say.

"And what is that, Mira?" He half-shutters his lids, expectant, perhaps wary.

"There you are!"

I turn to see Mother tramping toward us. She looks immediately at
Alejandro and hesitates only a moment before opening wide her arms.

"Ah, saved by your mother!" he says, and turns to embrace her. He knows it's inevitable, the questions, such as *are you really not married, and who is Mauricio other than your client?* They will have to wait.

"Alejandro, I would recognize you any where!"

"Hello, Mrs. Barnes!"

"I'm Margaret, please!"

"Yes, Margaret," he repeats, making her name sound like a confection of the highest quality, "What a wonderful pleasure."

"You have grown up, mister de la Torre," Mother says, returning in this moment to the time of her big adventure as an American woman living abroad.

"Not so much," he replies then leans in toward her as if confiding a secret. "I am still the boy you knew."

"Now why do I doubt that?" Margaret retorts, unintentionally touching upon the mystery of his presence, although I've said nothing to her about his Corrida clients. I wonder how Magill arrived at that bit of information about them being cartel. I suspect Mother will attempt to glean information about his current life in Cali with all the subtlety of a sledgehammer, although I recall the woman who, despite her tendency to dwell on the unpleasant, was admirably capable of sipping cocktails among the diplomatic and/or spy corps set in Tehran, Guatemala City, Cali.

My friends Donna and Gardner have arrived and since it's rare to find them on the west side, I leave Mother with Alejandro.

"Who is that man with your mother?" Donna immediately wants to know. My response is guarded. Now that he's being scrutinized by Margaret, he needn't be scrutinized by everyone.

"An old friend," I say, "A landscape designer."

"I figured you hadn't moved out of Venice," Donna says, "When I heard you were on the garden tour."

"Sorry I haven't been in touch."

"Don't be sorry," Gardner says, "We know how it is."

Being from the time of Charlie, these old friends conjure up the spirit of the man himself, and for a moment he stands but a breath away, a memory that breaks me in two. Suddenly a gust of ghostly breeze explodes across the eucalyptus in the canyon below, and I feel that tightening in my throat, the rush of warning. Alejandro watches me from over Mother's shoulder and concern floods his face but I look away, breathe deep, exhale slow.

Joined by Mother and Alejandro at the buffet table, I introduce Donna and Gardner to Alejandro and we all help ourselves to bites of crudities being passed by a caterer.

"This is delicious," Mother says.

"Is that the mushroom stuffed zucchini blossoms?" Donna says, "Aren't they fantastic?"

Margaret stops chewing. Her eyes seek rescue from me then, juggling plastic wineglass and paper plate and not a napkin to spit in within sight, Margaret valiantly, painfully, swallows what is undoubtedly a toadstool.

As expected, Mother is ready to go home fifteen minutes later. I tell her I can't leave as I need to speak with the head of Tour logistics about a nervous homeowner requiring additional docents. Alejandro politely offers to drive Margaret home and she leaps at the chance to exit the party with one of its more fascinating guests. I promise Mother I'll drop by if it isn't too late and wonder if he'll be there too, if he'll wait for me.

"Your mother is in my good hands," he says.

My radiantly girlish Mother looks like she's off on her first date with the King of the Prom. I speculate briefly on what kind of car he will be driving Mother home in, possibly one of those black Mercedes, and am certain that it won't disappoint her.

"That man yours?" Donna asks me as we watch them cross the lawn.

"I'm probably too 'mature' for him," I say.

"But," Gardner rejoins, "Didn't your mother say he was your high school boyfriend?"

"Oh, Gardner," says Donna, and she and I share a defiantly not-bitter laugh.

The rest of the evening is filled with speeches and words of praise for the gardens, homeowners, designers and contributors to the Neighborhood Youth Association, and every so often among the self-congratulatory preening a curious woman or two will ask me about "that man you were talking to." At the peak of the party, sometime between Magill holding court on a golden settee and his mugging before a phallic bloom springing from the giant "blue flame" *agave*, I find myself wondering if Alejandro is still at Mother's or if he's returned to the company of his international compatriots, never to be seen by me again.

"What are you waiting for?" says Magill the mind reader, suddenly standing beside me.

"I don't know," I reply, "Have I forgotten something or someone?"

"Oh, you haven't forgotten him," says Magill, "It's all you can do to keep from elevating over the pool."

"That obvious, huh?"

"Just get your shapely buttocks out of here and go get him before your mother scares him away."

— —

*"Look carefully before you pick a grape
from a cluster.
Black widow spiders live inside them and
you could die if one bit you."*

— —

I am approaching Mother's door, using my key to enter, when I hear laughter.

Mother's little house is ablaze with good cheer. A small fire flickers in the fireplace and her cats are stepping over the coffee table books and Alejandro's legs which are crossed at the knee, his finely tailored pants covered in cat fur and dust balls. Margaret is in her element with highball in hand, and he is sipping a glass of what appears to be white wine, although I didn't know Margaret had any in her 'fridge. He seems perfectly at ease among the newspapers billowing in little tents on the floor, the knitting, paints and photographs splayed on the coffee table.

"They'd taken a vote in Rosie's ninth grade class," Margaret is saying, "And they all thought you were dead except Rosie. She has ESP you know, and she turned out to be right!"

"Thank you, *Jesus*," he agrees. He sees me standing in the archway portico and stands to greet me.

"Si, muchas gracias Jesus," Mother rattles off. Like mine, Margaret's Spanish vocabulary is limited yet spoken rapidly and with a respectable accent, therefore to the casual non-speaker she appears impressively fluent.

"And I knew that if anyone could escape it would be you," she continues, without acknowledging my arrival.

"That was the official story yes, but when Papa was in hospital your husband kindly assisted with — "

"Did he? Dear Harry always wanted to play the hero," Margaret says, never one to miss an opportunity to denigrate her ex-husband, "Oh, hello Mira."

I wonder what Alejandro was about to say. Rumors circulated at the time that a ransom had materialized, and I wonder if my father had anything to do with that.

"Are you all right? How was your drive?" Mother asks, "Did you take Pacific Coast Highway?"

"It was fine," I reply too quickly, hoping Mother won't launch into the details of my freeway-driving phobia.

"Margaret, I must say goodnight." Alejandro stands. "And thank-you for your hospitality and your paciencia con migo."

"De nada, but don't tell me you're driving all the way back to Newport tonight?"

"Oh, I believe I must," he replies.

"But you've been drinking," Margaret protests then adds, "*Señor*," to lighten what might otherwise sound pejorative.

"Yes, but not so much, I am a good driver in all conditions, *Señora*."

Rather than offering that he sleep on her couch, Margaret looks from Alejandro to me and then him and back to me again and amazingly manages to say nothing.

⌐ ⌐

"Boys can do terrible things when their hormones kick in."

There are a number of reasons for inviting Alejandro back to my place, among them an impulse to show my childhood friend my home and the garden I have created. We enter the gate and walk the short path leading toward my cottage with its peeling paint and aromatic sages running wild around the gently trickling fountain. It is small, intimate, quietly reclusive, my garden, and he takes my hand, pulls me into the shadows beneath the *Buddleia davidii* and kisses me.

We kiss without moving, his palms locked against my hips, as if our mouths alone can express everything else our bodies want to do.

We do not talk; we can barely see each other in the dark. I stop him with a touch of my finger against his lips, and he takes a step back, waiting as I search for my keys until I realize they are in my hand. I can barely unlock the door; he has to steady my shaking hand. I laugh, I must laugh. Somehow the door is unlocked and we enter.

I don't know if I have managed to shut the door but I think he has done it. I hear it closing behind us, shutting the world out. He is unwrapping my tunic, running the silk across my breasts, pulling away my clothes. Again my hands shake when I work the buttons down the length of his shirt. I see the same chest but with more hair and darker, and as I unbuckle his belt I realize I've been unwittingly waiting for this for decades and I'm not about to wait a second longer, not to walk up the stairs, not to fall upon the bed in my room. I will make love finally with the one who should have been the first.

We are on the floor, and somewhere I hear moaning and realize it is my voice coming from deep in my throat. The wood floor is hard beneath me; I wrap my legs around him and reach back and hold onto the iron underside of the coffee table where I notice a small spider moving delicately into a corner. My breasts are scrubbed with his unshaven jaw, and it is all leaking out of me, thick and wet, tears and sweat. I clinch what I wanted so long ago, I don't want it to end – I want it to go on forever. I hold back until he murmurs *Mira* like a sigh, an anguished apology, and the warmth spreads through me. But it isn't over. He's not one to give up, patiently stroking until I am shaking beneath him, me whispering his name and pleading like a beggar without shame until I'm seized with the end.

Yes, I think, *old girlfriends are easy.*

— —

"If you have a funny feeling about someone, trust it. That person may be up to something"

The cats aren't happy to see a stranger in their bed, but Alejandro isn't aware of this. He stretches out on his back then turns over, hand propping his head, to look at me. He asks, está bien ahora? and I wonder if he remembers how it was in San Cipriano, how insane I had been, but I simply nod with a smile and mirror him, and in this position we talk, taking up where we left off, unable to stop until my eyes droop shut and I find myself sleeping in mid-conversation and feel his hand brushing my cheek.

We cover the high points of our decades apart. I tell him about Charlie. He watches me as if waiting for me to break down, but I tell him I'm cried out and he accepts this although it isn't entirely the truth. Nor do I mention Mother's weird warnings and my misgivings that Charlie's death proved her right or that I've been working with therapy and mindful thought to avoid being the walking fearful.

"What is it you want to know?" he asks. He is remembering that moment at Magill's when I had stepped back from him, that instant of my mistrust.

"So you're really not married?"

"No, Mira, I am not."

This seems impossible and again I sense him evading, and then he tells me she was murdered, his wife Maria, Mauricio's sister; that it happened ten years ago. They had no children and her death was not freakish and accidental like Charlie's but instead deliberate, targeted, part and parcel of his country's long and lawless civil war.

He rests his head back into the pillow and describes a paramilitary chief named Tinto demanding "protection" money then issuing demands for political favors. Finally, the last straw, there was the order that he be given land. But the land that goes back generations, sacrosanct for Maria's family and her brother Mauricio, this you never give away. It is the land your ancestors brought the cattle to graze in, the land you live in and love. You do not turn it over to a blackmailer nor do you give it to a killer. Because the Corridas said no to Tinto again and again, the family was punished with the life of Maria. She was shot while riding in the fields north of her family cattle ranch near Medellin.

"I have said many times to myself that we should have moved away," he says, "That I should not have allowed her to go home to the ranch. But that would be impossible. We do not run away from our country and leave it to the filth to take everything. This is what they want us to do and I won't allow it, never."

Alejandro closes his eyes. His face contorts for a moment then smoothes with a controlled effort. I am at a loss on what to say, and so I simply reach for his hand. Within seconds he is asleep. Staring at his face with impunity now, at the lines of expression, even in slumber, that have evolved from loss, I see rigid ferocity around the temples and jaw, a man for whom pain, rage and conviction have become an everyday thing, and for an instant it dawns on me that I've taken a stranger into my bed.

"Don't leave your house keys out
when strangers are around.
They can make clay impressions and break in
with duplicates."

I sleep fitfully, dream too much. In my dreams I see a woman on a horse. Her black hair flies in the wind and then that hair turns slick with blood and she falls from the horse into the beautiful land that is her native Colombia. Then that dark lush land of Colombia fades as I rise to consciousness and see the brilliance of California sun at my window.

Alejandro lies beside me gazing up at my attic ceiling. Winston glowers from his displaced position at the foot of the bed; Patrick and Darwin have made themselves scarce. Today looms full of responsibilities, being as it is the day of the Garden Tour, yet all I want is to remain here with him safe beside me while I ask the other question, the one that was forgotten when he told me of Maria's murder. Exactly who is Mauricio, I want to ask, although I suppose that question has already been answered: Mauricio is his brother-in-law and by that account always family.

Sensing me awake, he turns and catches me staring.

"You are awake now."

He runs has hand up my arm, and before I can calculate how he has artfully turned the full wattage of his charm in my direction he pins me under him and smiles down upon me, taking me slowly and with leisure until I want him, suspicion and caution be damned.

We are just beginning when I hear the thump-thudding sounds of cat feet and then something else, the slam of a door, the jangle of keys, and whatever warm running ecstasy I feel hardens to ice in an instant.

"Mira?" I hear the voice from downstairs, "Are you all right?"

He withdraws and rolls off me with a soft, gentle laugh, and I am tense with anger, so angry tears spring to my eyes.

"Es nada," he says.

"Mira! Aren't you up?"

Although I've given her the key to my house in case of emergencies, I've come to understand that every day is an emergency for Margaret. She won't be climbing up the steep stairway to my attic bedroom, but she stands at the base now, hollering up, again asking if I'm "all right."

I shout back "I hear you!" with more vehemence than necessary.

Alejandro is really laughing now, having a fine time of it. To him, Margaret is a generally congenial hard-drinking inquisitive and opinionated American mother. But I am fed-up, up-to-here fed-up, my morning orgasm denied me by none other than my mother.

"I'll make coffee," Margaret calls up, her voice tight but not exactly chagrined. She has heard his laughter and will attempt an air of sophisticated indifference.

"Brew a large pot!" I shout down.

We come down for breakfast together. I have chosen to wear a long white cotton dress today. Mother looks me over, and so I work the dress like a haughty fashion model while pouring coffee, heating croissants for the early tour visitors.

"Good morning, Margaret," Alejandro says.

"Hello," she coolly replies, turning away like a spurned lover.

He accepts a coffee from me and we exchange a glance.

"You are looking prepared for the tour today," he says, gesturing to the Kaminski raffia hat that hangs by a string down her back, "A lovely English woman to walk in her country garden."

"I'm an American," Mother says, "Not English."

Someone is ringing the bell and I go to the door to let in the docent who will be showing visitors my garden. Alejandro stays in the kitchen with Mother. I hear him telling her he's decided to join us on the tour, and when he does, Margaret announces she's staying at the house.

"But you will not be wanting to see the gardens your daughter has designed?"

When I return he looks uncomfortably toward me for help.

"I thought you were going on the tour, Mother," I say.

"I'm staying here."

I introduce the docent Sally who is dressed in a safari outfit.

"I love your garden!" she enthuses, "Orange poppies and sage and not a single weed!"

The thought of moody Mother spending the morning with this ebullient woman boggles the imagination.

"Mom, don't you want to see Julia's house?"

A famous actress's house and garden, designed by Magill, are on the Tour. Mother hoped to see it because the actress had been attacked by paparazzi at her back door and she wanted to see the spot where it happened.

Mother looks uncertain for a moment but sticks with her refusal. No housekeeper certainly, she's suddenly preoccupied with tidying up my already tidy kitchen, her movements proprietary, territorial.

"I am sorry that you are not coming with us," Alejandro says, "I will be returning to Newport this afternoon and then later flying back to Cali."

"Oh? When?" Her question is more an urgent request that he disappear, and it doesn't go unnoticed. His mouth turns down, the only indication that he is aware of her rudeness.

"Tomorrow, I am sorry to say." He slips his hands into the pockets of the trousers he wore last night which now look a little slouchier yet no less chic.

"Ah. Well. Bon voyage," she says, and jerks her chin in the air. It's quite a display of pouting, and I'm truly disgusted with her but not surprised. She seems to have forgotten that her daughter who fled the nest decades ago is no longer a teenager.

"Are you really leaving tomorrow?" I ask Alejandro as we step outside. There is a groan of frustrated anguish in my tone and he silently registers my displeasure with Mother's poorly timed entrance this morning by taking my hand and kissing it.

"Pobresita mi linda Mira," he says, "It is like we are teenagers again and your mother has caught us on the couch."

"Ha, ha!" I reply, the situation is too embarrassing for words.

We stand for a moment in my garden and watch as Juanita next door carefully steps down from her porch to water her garden. She waves to us across the fence. When I introduce her to Alejandro, her pale and papery one-hundred-year-old face beams upon him a warm gift of compensation for Mother's rudeness. Alejandro returns her *buenos dias* then, ignoring Margaret glowering from the open doorway, turns to me, shakes his head, and again gently attempts to reassure me with, "Es nada, no problema, mi amor."

"You can drown without a sound."

We join garden and architectural tourists walking and biking from site to site; the gardeners, the curious, the affluent couples calculating plans for their multi-million renovations. The words "sustainability" and "eco friendly" are referenced with near religious fervor.

"We have many of these *heliconia* in my country," Alejandro says of the tropical "lobster claw" plant.

"These are 'Hot Lips,'" I say pointing to tiny red and white bicolor flowers.

"*Perdóname?*"

"Well, it's *salvia microphylla*, if you must know."

"I think I prefer the other name," he says, then adds, "*Sedum rupestre*" in reference to a lime green groundcover bursting from broken concrete.

"*Lavandula stoechas*," I say before a sweep of Spanish lavender.

"*Achillea millefolium*," he whispers into my ear.

"*Coitus interruptus*," I reply, recalling this morning's inanity. He laughs and slips his hand in mine.

"This is good," he says at the Neighborhood Youth Association's Children's Center, "It is like my biblioteca in Barranquilla where the city businesses fund the building of the rooms, and now it is much better for the children."

A boy explains the process of decomposition at the composting bin. I watch Alejandro nodding encouragingly, standing in the apex of a trio of Kaminski-hatted ladies. Suddenly he pats his pockets, says he left his phone in the car, and asks if he may use mine. I say *of course,* and hand over my iPhone. Stepping toward a trickling fountain on the other side of the tomato patch, he touches and scrolls through my mobile, talks quickly, appears to be leaving a message. The Kaminski-hatted ladies appraise him from under their brims. I pull a cloth hat from my bag and put it on my overheated head.

The afternoon grows warm and breezy and the horizon dissolves into the milky turquoise of a Diebenkorn. An old unease creeps back until I identify it as hunger. Hungry for lunch and, now that I think of it, hungry for Alejandro. Ideally, this is the point at which I drag him by the hair to my cave, but my sanctuary is being overseen by a perky docent, gloomy Mom, and hundreds of garden enthusiasts tromping through my sustainable garden. Unlike my garden, I don't feel in the least sustainable, but rather cravenly wanting.

We walk to the Boardwalk, grab a take-out lunch and screw-top bottle of chilled white wine, and head down to the water's edge. I pour the wine into plastic cups, gulp it like Kool-aid, and attempt to satiate my desire with doughy premade sandwiches. Alejandro talks of his landscapes in places like Sri Lanka, Madagascar, Rio de Janiero, Quitos, but my unspoken questions are *When are you coming back? When will I see you again?* I take off my shoes, lie back and grasp and turn sand between my fingers and toes, as if by the mixing and churning of sand my free-range lust will dissipate. I can't stop it, this unsettling dissatisfaction. Like a once-dormant volcano reawakened, I am ready to explode. Although I'm constrained by some inner dictum to act like a grown woman instead of some hormonal teen, I'm reminded me of how I was before grief made me drought tolerant, and what I crave now is torrential rain.

Alejandro lies beside me, looks up at the sky. He runs his finger across my wrist. "Your mother," he says with a sigh, "She visits you often?"

"Define visits."

"Ah. She is there often and this you do not like."

"No, I do not like, that's for sure."

It's tempting to suggest that we check into a hotel. Never do I recall being so impatient for more lovemaking, my only excuse, if excuses are required, being that I've been celibate for two years. And something else: a nagging memory that hounds me. I wonder if he truly remembers the details of the day we ran away to San Cipriano.

"My flight leaves tomorrow for Bogota, early, I am sorry."

Suddenly he stands, pulls me to my feet and gives me the look-of-the-hooded-eyes.

"Come with me."

For a moment I mistake his meaning, for that is precisely what I want.

"Come with me to Cali."

"You want me to fly back to Cali with you?" The suggestion seems so improbably impulsive and romantic.

"I will take you to *Club Campestre,*" he whispers, "I will carry you through the olive garden like before only I cannot promise that it will end only with kisses."

"Colombia," I say, "Fly with you to Cali." It's like he's asking me to jet into outer space.

"And why not? What is to stop you, Mira Barnes?"

The tide reaches toward our feet and I feel a touch of vertigo.

"I can't, really," I say, and don't add the truth, which is that I can't endure the thought of being inside an airplane for however long it takes to get there, not even if plied with champagne the entire way.

"Por qué no?"

"Well," I say, grasping for a reason not to follow this man to the ends of the earth, "I've — I've got to take Mother to visit Rosie, for one. And I hate to fly. I'm somewhat of a coward about it," I add.

"Not Mira Barnes."

"Not Mira Barnes? And why not Mira Barnes? Alejandro, you don't know the half of it."

"What half is that? You will fly sin problemas and I will take you on a garden tour of my Colombia where we have the most beautiful gardens on earth. We will see the Amazonia. We will swim in rivers as we did in San Cipriano. Remember San Cipriano?"

I wonder what he actually does remember about San Cipriano.

"We ran away," I prompt.

We skipped school. He waited for me at the bus stop and before he saw me approaching I watched him, a slim youth in jeans and blue workman's shirt, shoulder bag for a day trip at his side, staring off in concentrated thought until I stepped into his field of vision. His face lit up and I could feel it on my face too, his joy and ours, our mutual recognition that we were friends in love. I heard the song playing *come Saturday morning I'm going away with my friend* only it wasn't Saturday, it was a school day, and we were running away.

We held hands on the rickety old bus. In my small backpack I'd brought everything I thought I would need: Bonnie Bell make-up, a towel, swimsuit, and, most importantly, a condom I had begged off of Connie Quevedo, who said it wouldn't hurt if I was "horny," a word I hated. On the bus the radio was playing Jose Feliciano's rendition of "Fool On the Hill" which I said I liked best though Alejandro said I was crazy, the Beatles' version was better.

What I remember most when we got there wasn't the wild railcar ride to a tiny village in the heart of the tropical rainforest, or how we tire-rafted down the river and swam under waterfalls. What I remember is a warm rainstorm sending us swimming for cover in the eddies of a water-hole beneath the mangroves and how wet kisses led to the removal of my swimsuit and all that followed.

"You were a wild girl, Mira," Alejandro says to me now.

So he remembers.

"I wanted you," I say, "and you said no. The girl is the one who is supposed to say no."

The condom turned out to be punctured and mangled inside its cheap foil casing, even though I'd slipped it carefully into a paperback copy of Neruda's *The Captain's Verses,* marking my favorite, "Night On the Island." I wanted to lose my virginity, protection be damned, but he was unwilling to go further, choosing to be responsible when what I wanted was to be ravaged. As it turned out, I was ravaged, just not how I'd expected to be.

"Did I not satisfy you?" Alejandro asks me now on the beach in Venice, and together we are back in the rainforest:

The river flowed around us as we had pulled our tire tubes together among the mangrove roots. I was captured, entangled. He coaxed me, kissed me down the length of my body, rose up my pelvis on the floating tube and whispered soft encouragements until I opened like a hothouse flower. *Come on,* I said, pulling at him, hard smooth and beautiful, but he wouldn't, and with his tongue he brought me to the cusp, naked and floating against the vines, me nearly drowning him, grasping, pulling at his hair, and then crying afterwards, embarrassed and angry.

"You satisfied me alright," I say.

"You were — shy," he says and smiles, a grown-up recalling a child, "But how could I forget the first woman I loved in that way?"

I too never forgot.

I had demanded the quick recovery of my bathing suit. I said I'd been humiliated, for I had given myself over to him in a way I didn't understand. *Didn't you like it?* he'd said afterwards. *It wasn't normal,* I replied, *why can't we do it the normal way,* and then I said, *I think you're mean.* It was ecstasy, but the crazy kind. He made me crazy and I thought of how I might want more, but didn't say, because he had made me crazy, crazed, mad, and so I demanded that it be his turn, and he smiled and showed me how, shocking me with the stream of milky liquid while he sighed and laughed and said, *esta bien, muy bien, Mira.*

We returned to Cali, me silent on the bus when Feliciano sang "Light My Fire," him watching me between glances out the window at the meadows and cattle. When he dropped me at home in the *colectivo* I didn't kiss him but instead walked away without saying good-bye, back into my house, to the cruel words Mother dished out in those days which, this time after my runaway adventure, were exceptionally inspired: *"I wish you'd never been born. My hands have grown old wringing out your diapers. You'll be pregnant before you're nineteen."*

The next day at school I ignored him, heard him laughing with his soccer teammates, convinced he was talking about me, rejecting me. Being Margaret's tough daughter, I would reject him first, show I wasn't overwhelmed by him, though clearly I was. I returned home on the school bus to study for the SATs while he played in the soccer match, witnessed the near fatal shooting of his father and was abducted and held prisoner by the *Fuerzas Armadas Revolucionarias de Colombia.*

In the months he was missing and presumed to be dead I listened in the night to the whistle of the security man on the bicycle circling our house and thought of how frightened he must have been and how an unrequited teenage romance didn't matter much to others.

"It was a horrible thing that happened to you," I now say on our walk along Venice Beach. He doesn't respond, and so I say, "I wanted you so much then and now look at me, I still want you."

"Ah Mira, then we must solve este problema."

He grasps the back of my neck, looks at me for a moment, and gives me a kiss that is meant to solve the situation.

"Este problema," I repeat. The tide swirls up around our feet. The hem of my dress is wet and clings against my calves.

"I — my country — we are still in trouble, Mira."

The words, spoken softly, come out of the blue.

"What do you mean?"

He shrugs, an attempt to lighten his troubling remark.

"It is a long story, and always the same. Too much has changed in my country. Perhaps we should again run away. We could fly up and disappear forever into the ceiba trees."

"What are you saying? What do you mean, disappear?"

He pulls his sunglasses from his pocket, holds them up to the sun and cleans them with the edge of his shirt.

"The San Cipriano we knew is forever vanished," he says, "There is gold fever and international mines by the river now and people are killing each other. It is how it is in my country. Not always, of course, it is better in some ways, but not good, still not good."

"Are *you* in trouble?"

His puts on the sunglasses. Ray Bans. His lips form the facsimile of a small, tight, smile.

"No. I am not in trouble."

He is lying.

"Can I just ask you one more thing?"

"One thing? Yes, Mira. Ask me one thing."

He waits, facing me in his unyielding Ray Bans.

"I just want to ask —" I hesitate, the question heavy on my tongue, "What does Mauricio do?"

"Do?"

"For a living. Magill said something about —"

"He is a coffee exporter."

He lifts up his sunglasses and looks at me full on when he says this, so that I can see this is not a lie. It's a line. We both know it's the official line. And because he looks at me this way, frank, dead on with naked eyes, I know he is not lying to me.

Our private language has spanned time, violence and culture; he answers me with the official line, and so I nod my acceptance. And then he drops the sunglasses back down over his eyes and I wrap my arm around his waist and together we walk back up the sand away from the sea.

"If you're feeling anxious it's your instinct telling you something is wrong."

On our walk back to his car he asks if I'm in touch with anyone from *Colegio Bolivar*. Old friends, old acquaintances? I say no. There was a reunion a while ago, he says, although few Americans attended. Mostly the locals, but they too have moved on, joining UNESCO, traveling on to Europe.

"What about that friend of your father's from Uniroyal?" Alejandro asks, "What was his name. Dennis? The swimmer."

"Oh yeah. He came to Father's memorial. He was younger than my dad. He's around in his sixties or seventies now."

"Nice man," he says vaguely.

I am annoyed by our chattiness, an attempt to cool down and act like old acquaintances.

We approach one of the black Mercedes I saw from the fleet, parked in the alleyway behind Mother's house where he left it the night before. A eucalyptus has dropped nuts down onto the windshield, and as we stand under the filigree of a low sweeping branch Alejandro offhandedly remarks that the Mercedes is not Mauricio's but rather belongs to a friend who is "renowned in certain circles of the rich," this being but one of the many cars he keeps in places all over the world. I ask who this man is, but he isn't forthcoming and merely says he is "just some banker with a private jet."

More questions hang in the air, but it is time to say good-bye. I want him to take off the sunglasses, it's nearing late afternoon after all, but he doesn't.

"Do you know what it is for a flower to be anonymously extinct?" he asks me. "It is when it is never known to botanists and disappears from the forest forever without ever being known. That is what will happen to you if you do not come with me."

It is a ludicrously machismo remark but flattering nonetheless to hear him so assiduously pressing his case.

"What a Victorian way of saying I'll become an old maid."

"Mira, you will never be old to me."

I want to add that he isn't my only salvation but can't say at this moment that it's true. Will I become so *drought tolerant* that I won't even know how much I'm capable of doing without?

"Come with me to Cali."

He puts his hands on my waist and turns me so my back is against the warm surface of the Mercedes. He whispers in Spanish that he wants a rain check for what was denied us this morning. I strap my fingers into his belt; pull his hips toward mine. The alleyway is deserted, and I can hear the distant barking of dogs and the muted voices of garden tourists a block away.

"How can I persuade you," he says.

I am cocooned against the car, its warm steel on my back. He lifts the hem of my dress and I feel his hand moving along the thin fabric of my underwear. A brief movement of his fingers demonstrates with considerable accuracy only the beginning of precisely what lays in store for me should I accompany him back to his native Colombia. I look over his shoulder, past his unsmiling lips and sunglasses. He gives me only a taste of what I could have and slowly a smile forms upon his lips and he removes his hand and smoothes the skirt of my dress back down.

"That was cruel," I say, and I too smile since it's actually pretty funny, how he thinks he can taunt and provoke me this way.

He pushes me roughly against the car and gives me a kiss that feels more like a fuck, his tongue wrapping mine.

"Come with me," he commands.

My hands rub over his hardening crotch but he pulls them up to his chest and holds them there.

"Aquí no, cara mia. Pero en Cali, si," he promises, "Muchísimo."

We take a breath. It's a standoff. I see one of Mother's cats watching me from her kitchen window.

"Despues, si," I say. It's an affirmation of what I must do to have more of him. I will fly. I will risk life, limbs, sanity. *Why not?* I ask, *Why can't I have him?*

"Si," I say again, unwilling to let go of this second chance. I will have him beside me, in Venice or the world, this third act in my five-act play.

"Yes?" He releases me, and steps back. If I could view his eyes through the Ray Bans I suspect I would see triumph.

"I'm taking Mother to see Rosie in Michigan first. But in a week or two, I will come see you. Está bien?"

"Bien," he says. "Do not forget your passport."

Pack my passport, pack it right away.

"I will show you los delfines rosados de Amazonia."

The pink dolphins of the Amazon. What my father never had a chance to see.

"I've always wanted to go to the Amazon," I say, "I can't believe I'm going to do it."

"Remember. You are Harry Barnes' daughter."

Yes. Forget fear of flying. Forget fear period. Instead, try life.

━ ～

"If you have a suspicious feeling about someone, trust your instincts.

Jeffrey Dahmer was nice and charming right up until he strangled his victims."

"What do you know about Alejandro, really?"

The docent has left, but there are a few remaining stragglers exploring my little garden patch on their own. I choose not to respond to Mother's question because I suspect that at the moment I'd be somewhat irrational on the subject. What can I say? *I know nothing about him except what I feel?* My position is perfectly indefensible, but then, there's no requirement for me to defend or justify myself, either to my mother or anyone else for that matter. It's not that I'm necessarily putting my trust in the man but rather investing my interest in his welfare. I'm going on gut instinct — *my instinct.* Playing it safe is not in the cards, and it's a complete contradiction to all I've been taught.

I shed my walking shoes, slip into flip-flops, shake damp sand from the hem of my skirt and sweep it into a dustbin. Before I forget I find my passport in a box in the back closet, still current after a shoot in Rome five years ago, and slip it into my bag.

In the living room I settle into a favorite old rocker and prop my bare feet up on the coffee table. Knowing her way around my kitchen, Margaret makes two Bombay tonics, hands me one, and sits on the deco couch I salvaged from an alley in Brentwood. The gin and tonic fizzes at my nose and tastes great, even without the lime, which Mother hasn't bothered to add. When Margaret is ready to have a drink, she doesn't fuss with the details.

"Alejandro is very charming and sophisticated," she persists, "He always was a very *proper* young man. But what do you know about him really?"

"Not much," I say, taking the path of least resistance by refusing to engage. Margaret will be how she will be, and there is no stopping her from the drama she's in the process of creating.

She swills down the rest of her drink, sets the moist glass down on my mahogany coffee table.

"Really Mira, I don't know how you can say that. Your recent behavior concerning this man is shockingly inappropriate."

"Seriously? Seriously, Mother?"

I pick up Margaret's glass before it can create a permanent watermark, rise, and hold out my hand.

"I think it's time I took my house keys back."

"What?"

In the heartbeat of my request her expression shifts from octogenarian matriarch to cornered child. She has gotten herself in tricky territory. The Greatest Generation rarely discusses sexuality with the Boomer Generation that has found its own way and made its own rules, and all I know is that this mother-daughter tango cannot continue. Mother has slipped the thin edge of the wedge of her uncannily paranoid influence into my adult life in these past two years of my greatest vulnerability, even though I never asked her to move to California, let alone right up the street. I wonder why she is so intent on having me be dependent. Could it be that she resents me for being the younger woman, the rival who also happens to be her daughter? Daughters are younger than their mothers, an unfortunate fact of life.

I realize now that I absolutely must fly Mother to Rosie in Michigan. Let Rosie deal with her. Let Johan get off the couch and entertain her. Jonathan can show Grandma his latest superhero collection. And maybe I will board a flight for Cali.

"My house keys," I repeat, "You entered my home without ringing or knocking this morning Mother, and you know you shouldn't have done that."

"But I was concerned for you!" She's all wide-eyed innocence. "I was worried you would miss the tour!"

"Come on. You weren't concerned or worried, you were just meddling."

"I was *not* meddling. The last thing I expected to see was some Colombian drug lord emerging from your bedroom!"

She explodes off the couch, her voice trembling in a facsimile of self-righteous indignation.

"You don't know that about Alejandro. In fact your allegation is absurd," I say. Although Alejandro indicated just this afternoon that his brother-in-law Mauricio "*imports coffee,*" I'm not about to share this with the most paranoid person I know.

And besides, there is something in Father's past having to do with Colombia which Margaret has kept secret. I'm almost certain of that now, but if I ask about it I'll undoubtedly get a skewed answer, one that will turn the full bore of her bitterness against the man she divorced and the father I loved.

"Just give me my house key, please."

Margaret picks up the tote she perpetually lugs from her house to mine. I think she's about to dig inside for the keys, but no, she slings the bag onto the crook of her arm and prepares to take her leave.

"Aren't you forgetting something?" I ask.

She turns to look at me, confused for a second, and I wonder if she's growing more forgetful.

"My keys." I hold out my hand. "Keys," I say again.

"But what if something happens and I can't get in?" Mother says, "What if you fall coming down those awful steps or you leave on the gas or toxic fumes from —"

"Let's not think about that right now," I say. What I really should say is, *I'm not going to fall or leave on the gas.*

Margaret wades through her tote for the keys, pauses in frustration, then in a dramatic gesture worthy of farce upends the entire bag and lets everything roll, bounce and flutter across the floor. The cats scatter. She stands defiant, hands on hips, as if she's made some fantastic statement. It used to terrorize us, Rosie, Father and me, seeing a grown woman acting this way, but it was her way of manipulating and controlling. *You all think I'm an old witch,* she would say. Father would respond with reserve and kindness and Rosie and I would say, *no, Mother, we don't think you're a witch,* even though we did. Looking at her now, this difficult old lady with her white punk hairdo, I suspect our enabling only fueled her resentment as she attempted to exert some control.

I bend at her feet and find in the scattered jumble her keys dangling from the silver Dior pendant. I slide my house key off the ring and gather up all her things, her prim DKNY wallet, an imitation Hermes scarf, today's Calendar section from the Times, the latest Ann Rule novel, the tidy little make-up bag containing everything from lipstick to drugs, and put it all back in her bag as she stands there, imperious.

"I want *my* keys back too," Mother says.

"Does this mean we're breaking up?"

She huffs as I locate my own keychain in the ceramic bowl on the stand by my front door. I peel her key off and hand it back, but as she steps toward the door she suddenly stops and turns. Her shoulders sag just a fraction.

"Are you coming over for dinner later?" she asks.

This is another trait of hers: The tendency to create drama then moments later act as if nothing has happened.

"Ah, I don't think so, not tonight, Mother."

She nods and steps outside to the people still lingering in my garden.

And then she's suddenly friendly, pausing to talk on the walkway to the tourists admiring the blooming *buddleia davidii*, accepting their praise of my miniscule garden as though it were hers alone.

Anonymous Extinction

—   —

*"They say it's turbulence so you won't worry
but by the time you realize something's wrong
it's too late."*

—   —

I haven't flown with Mother since I was fifteen but her grim expression takes me into the way back machine to when Rosie and I returned with her to the U.S., leaving Father alone in Cali. Father considered travel an adventure; Mother saw it as traumatic; and for their daughters relocation meant spiraling death from the sky.

The businessman seated to Mother's left casts wary glances at her from his laptop as every other dip in the plane's motion prompts an esophageal groan of sincerely sickened terror. Margaret is in the middle seat, I at the window. I need only observe her clutching the armrest, face grimacing, to conclude she must be singlehandedly keeping the plane up. No one wants to indulge her fear, me least of all, and so I close my eyes and pretend sleep while wondering if my stomach cramps are due to the bag of packaged airline peanuts or symptoms of ovarian cancer.

I've undergone the yearly check-ups, Mother's breast cancer of over thirty years ago having put Rosie and me in the high-risk category. I fret over the recent BRCA blood test and their results, pending within the week. Do they tell you on the phone that you're genetically prone to breast cancer or do they just leave a message on voicemail? And while I'm at it, what's with this ringing in my ears and is it true what some experts say, that cellphones cause brain cancer? I'm alternately hyper and exhausted, which could mean some neurological problem. Not Chronic Fatigue Syndrome but more like Sporadic Hyperactivity and Fatigue Syndrome. The blood tests, ultra sounds and yearly mammograms and MRIs may seem excessively diligent by some standards, not to mention expensive, but I'd rather be neurotic and alive than normal and dead.

The plane jostles again and my heart leaps somewhere into the vicinity of my throat. I take a calming breath, ignore Mother's groan. I think of Alejandro, and after exhausting my review of our one-night tryst I recall his graciously effusive phone call on the day he left Los Angeles in which he thanked me for our time together, again urging me to visit. I haven't given him the exact date of my arrival, let alone bought a ticket, but I pull up his subsequent text and read it again.

Come to me, mi Mira.

I'm possessed by a tug of desire that says *remember what it is to be alive? Well, this is it. Welcome back to the living.*

The plane does another big bump then an abrupt sinking. *Welcome back to the living,* I think, *only to die on this flight.* Mother's nostrils make a series of shrill honking sounds as deep intakes of air rush past her beleaguered adenoids. The plane shudders and settles only to sink again, and soon the pilot comes on to warn us we'll be going through a "bumpy patch" on our approach to Detroit. This means for Mother and me that we should assume crash-landing positions. I reach for my glass of white zinfandel, my own sinuses clogged from wine histamine and cabin pressure, and recall

Dr. I's suggestion to imagine myself at the controls in the cockpit. The notion of this is vaguely comforting until I hear Margaret's strangled sob and all my therapy goes crash landing into the Midwestern cornfields below. When she starts rapidly panting like dehydrated pooch, the businessman leans forward to give me a look of concern. I manage a crooked smile and in semi-inebriated silence I turn to stare out the window into the dark sky.

The pilot comes back on to ominously inform us of tornado warnings. Beverage service is cut off. I swill the rest of my zinfandel; Mother clutches her sweating gin and tonic. The flight attendants are strapping down in their seats. The plane is quiet. Is everyone thinking the same thing? As in, *"we're all gonna die"*?

The plane lurches wildly and tears course down my cheeks. *Oh why oh why couldn't we have had a perfect weather day? Why us? Why?*

I grip Mother's hand and with the other I page through *Garden Design* and stare at a feature story on a landscape I designed with Magill and wonder if this is it, if my friends will say at least she had some success before she died. I think of how Rosie has all but murdered me, getting me onto this flight. I think of how Alejandro and I made love just that one night only to have Mother spoil our morning-after. I could strangle her now if she weren't already going to die in the seat beside me.

The plane does a big jolting dive and I see lightning cutting through the purple sky. Mother's drink slides off her tray and into the lap of the businessman, but she doesn't even notice. He politely brushes off remnants of gin and ice from his pants without saying a word. Her fingernails are digging into my hand, but I don't feel it as pain, only contact. The wings are shuddering horribly and we sink down through what feels like miles of clouds.

Somewhere in the back of the plane I hear a middle-aged learning-disabled man expressing mild concern: "Uh-oh," he says, his pitch sonorous but boyish. "Uh-huh," says another disabled man traveling with the chaperoned home group. They giggle nervously, a chorus of "uh-ohs." They could be climbing to the top of a roller coaster ride, their voices no more than mildly nonplussed. I envy their innocence.

When I see the wings bending and swear they're going to rip right off, I begin praying and clutching my crystal talisman, but my words are nonsensical and repetitive, something like *please God please God*, and in the middle of this repetition I have but one thought and that is to see Alejandro again.

We sink through the dark clouds and suddenly I see the runway looming up, fifty feet below, ten, and then we touch down, the wheels bouncing on slick Tarmac. We're going to live!

Everyone cheers. The flight attendants are back on their feet and hastily moving down the aisle to pick up drinks and trash. The pilot is thanking us for traveling with them as though it were a perfectly ordinary flight, *as if we didn't nearly crash and burn together in a fiery inferno.*

In hysterical relief I think of how my crystal talisman saved me.

Mother suddenly lets go my hand, literally shakes it loose.

"Are you ALL RIGHT?" she shouts. Her eyes are open now and she's turning to look at me, her face close.

"What about you?" I say, but Mother has already turned away from me to speak to the businessman and explain:

"My daughter's afraid of flying."

＊

*"When you're outside during a tornado
fall instantly to the ground and lie flat or
you'll get blown apart."*

＊

Jonathan is screaming and running up and down the basement stairs. The cats crouch, ears back, as he runs roughshod over them. His terrier Benji follows, toenails clattering on wood, up and down, down and up, knocking over bowls of cat kibble that have been inexplicably placed in front of the stairway. Mother has offered to "help" Rosie by feeding the cats yet has strangely placed the cat dishes in the center of the action.

"Mother, please, could you move the cats' dishes please?"

Rosie's double-please underscores the room's tension. She and Johan are cooking a paella for our first night in Ann Arbor, which means they haven't had time to sit down to relax after a full workday, and for this reason Rosie seems put out. A bucket of take-out chicken would have been fine with me, but Rosie is determined to do something special for us even if it really pisses her off.

Our guest rooms have been beautifully decorated with special touch-es — vases of delicate flowers fresh-picked from her garden, plush guest towels and high quality soaps, turned-down linens and quilts. Mother's accommodations are upstairs; mine are in the basement converted to look like a French country inn, although the litter boxes for Rosie's seven cats lining one wall emit a toxic ammonia scent. This seriously ruins the ambience but the smelly litter boxes remain, an apparent stand off issue with Jonathan whose job it is to clean them.

"We *have* to go down to the basement now!" Jonathan yells. He's standing on the top stair and glaring at us in the kitchen, a look of genu-ine panic on his face.

"Jon boy, the tornado is over," Johan says.

"It is *not*. I haven't heard the all clear!"

"Maybe that's because you're indoors," I suggest.

Jonathan gives me a "do-I-know-you?" look.

"Jonathan, give your Auntie Mira a kiss hello then go clean the litter boxes."

"NO!"

"Jonathan doesn't have to kiss me," I say.

My mind wanders to how I'm going to say it: *Thanks everyone and sorry for the brief visit, but I've gotta go to Colombia to see my lover. Yes, lover. Aunt Mira has a lover.*

"You can give your *Grandma* a kiss," Margaret volunteers and holds her arms wide. She's working hard to get on Rosie's good side and succeeds for a moment when Jonathan demonstrates his power by rushing into her arms.

"I guess some people just don't have the mommy gene," Margaret says to no one in particular. Jonathan whines and squirms in her arms.

"Please, Grandma, we've got to take cover!" says the seven-year old tyrant.

"Jonathan has learned a lot about what to do in emergencies, haven't you Jonathan?" Mother says.

Rosie slams the Sabatier through a mushroom with more force than necessary.

"You're not supposed to sit under a tree in a storm," Jonathan says.

"And don't walk under icicles," Mother says, "because one can fetch lose and —"

"Never mind that for now," Rosie interrupts.

"We've explained to Jonathan that nothing bad can happen if you act intelligently," Johan says, "Isn't that right, son?"

"But you never know –" Margaret begins.

"Mother, let's not confuse the issue," Rosie says.

"What? What?" Jonathan wants to know.

"Your Grandmother likes to take into account worst case scenarios," Johan says.

Margaret studies her delicately veined hand laid flat on the wide maple chopping block and looks sufficiently chastised for me to feel sorry for her.

A light rain flutters against the kitchen window but the storm's intensity has passed and it appears to be clearing. Through the back window I think I see the spark of a firefly, a fairytale invitation to a memory of the Ohio farm where Father grew up. Jonathan looks like the pictures of his granddad when he was his age, although I think the facial expressions are different: Father in his boyhood pictures had a creased brow like Charlie Brown's, whereas Jonathan is a child of perpetual laughter and light. Except, that is, when terrified by potential death-by-tornado.

"Mira has a new beau," Mother says. Johan and Rosie raise eyebrows in unison.

"What's a bo?" asks Jonathan.

"It's a boyfriend," Rosie says, not looking at me, her attention on her cooking, "Who is it?"

"Not a boyfriend, really," I say, "Mother's exaggerating."

"Oh, you mean Alejandro," Rosie says, "He was always more grown up than the rest of us. But he was just breezing through town, wasn't he?"

What I hear is, *he has no interest in you.*

"That's right," I say, "Just breezing through."

Rosie reaches for a colander and asks me to help her pick lettuce. I follow outside into her wet Michigan garden. The night air is warm and humid and I am reminded that just hours ago I was in dry Los Angeles, thousands of miles from this fertile Midwestern land. I can practically smell the oat and cornfields of our grandfather's farm.

I quietly relish Rosie's presence beside me as we step along the garden border in our faded jeans and tanks. We pick, snip and drop leaves into the colander. We are blood and more than blood, for we have traveled far together.

"Mom's already got Jonathan going." Rosie says, "He's never this way with other guests."

"You mean this tornado thing? They both seem to love it."

"Are you kidding? He's terrified, can't you see?"

Maybe he's pulling your chain, I think but don't say. Instead I stand up for a moment to stretch my back and watch the fireflies drift up – up – into the trees.

"Why didn't you tell me she's getting worse?" Rosie says.

"The tornado stuff's always the same."

"No, I mean her balance, her hearing. And she's drinking more."

"Well it's been a couple years, Rosie. She's older and more fragile. I told you that."

"But these symptoms are disturbing. Her balance, especially. And she's not hearing me."

"She's never been a good listener."

"You're in denial here."

"No, I've just seen her change gradually. To you it's a shock."

"We need to do an intervention on her drinking."

"What?"

This seems radical to me. *What will it change,* I think, *and is her drinking really that bad?* It will not go down well and Margaret will resist with every inch of her formidable backbone.

"She's got to start using a cane. She almost fell down in my driveway."

"Well, if you think an intervention will force her to use one –"

"I mean on her drinking."

"Why don't you tell her that, as a doctor, you think she should cut back a little."

"Right, put it all on me!"

"All on you! I've been practically living with her! You haven't seen her in two years!"

"You didn't say she was this bad."

"She's just getting older."

"It's not just age."

"You're the doc, so fine. It's not age, if you say so."

"Okay. Fine."

"Fine."

We pause for a moment. I try to relax and take it all in, the delphiniums drooping and wet over the peonies, the mist in the air.

"Before she moved to California I was always driving over to her place on my days off," Rosie says, "To clean up cat hair and mop her floors."

"Well thanks to you, I do it now."

"I clean up after my boys," Rosie retorts, "I didn't need Mother too."

"Well at least you have Jonathan and Johan. I lost Charlie and Father and now I'm Mom's cleaning lady."

"He was my father too you know."

"I know."

We drop that landmine of a subject. We are possessive of our dead father as only the children of a hateful divorce can be.

"What are you girls talking about out there?"

Mother's silhouette is at the back kitchen doorway and I see her gripping the doorframe for balance. Rosie takes in an exhausted breath of — exasperation? frustration? — as she gathers up the colander of arugula and lettuce. She stares across the lawn at Jonathan, who is jumping up and down beside his hunched grandmother.

"Rosie," I say, "I could take a load off you, do your grocery shopping tomorrow while you're at work then pick Jonathan up from camp."

"No, that's alright," Rosie says, "You wouldn't know what we need —"

"Hurry, Mommy!"

"Really," I press on, "I could at least pick up Jonathan, we could —"

"Coming honey," Rosie calls out, then says to me without looking my way and in so quick and surprising a manner I wonder if I've heard her right: "He's my son, not yours."

"*Always sleep with an open window to avoid asphyxiation from toxic fumes.*"

At four a.m. in the bed beside the fumy cat-litter boxes in the otherwise beautifully decorated basement guest room of my sister's house, I review the evening. I think of how adept Rosie, Margaret and I are in the art of interpersonal conflict, how our consistent *modus operandi* revolves around inevitably pitting one of us against the other two. Never are we three in agreement in this constantly shifting triangle in which one of us becomes the target the other two set upon.

He's my son, not yours. Rosie has a point, but it's not like I was planning to kidnap him. I barely know how to talk to children. Maybe this is why she doesn't trust me to be with Jonathan.

Some of us just don't have the mommy gene. I must give her credit. Mother knows how to align herself with the other mommy in the room.

What was it that Alejandro said about plants unknown to man becoming anonymously extinct? He was referring to flowers. And I am one such flower that has failed to reproduce.

My stomach cramps and as I breathe through the ache I recall the pamphlet in my gynecologist's office listing the illusive symptoms of ovarian cancer, one of which is feelings of doom. And I *do* feel doomed, left with these intractable cat ladies while Father and Charlie took with their passing all that was joyful. I worry about the BRCA test then decide it's just the paella. The pain subsides. I rise up to sip from a bedside water glass and then pick bits of cat dander off my tongue.

One of Rosie's cats jumps to a shelf above the dryer, and that's when I see it, crammed between laundry detergent and medical journals, a dusty family artifact awaiting anonymity at a garage sale:

The bronze box that holds Father's ashes.

Not that Rosie would sell Father's ashes at a garage sale or anyone would buy them, but is this really where his remains should be? Here among the someday giveaways, the cheap knickknacks and records we no longer listen to? Rosie had insisted on keeping his ashes in the same way she sought to preserve the family valuables following the wreckage of our parents' divorce, and now that Father is gone Rosie would have him, or at least his ashes. Before returning to their home in Hawaii, Gloria entrusted her husband's remains to Rosie on the condition that his daughters would agree on a burial location. Fat chance on that.

"Why not a proper cemetery or park?" I had suggested when Rosie said we should bury Father under her back yard cherry tree, "I mean, what happens if you sell your house?"

"We'll never sell the house," Rosie said.

"But you don't know that."

"This is where Jonathan grew up. He loves this house. We can bury Father alongside Gigi and Ringo."

"But Gigi and Ringo are cats!"

"We loved them too. You loved Ringo!"

"That doesn't mean I want to bury Father with Ringo in your fucking backyard pet cemetery."

"You don't need to curse at me."

"I just said fuck. I wasn't cursing *at* you."

"Don't ever speak to me in that tone of voice."

We were given a reprieve from any further discussion of Father's burial site as life, or rather, another death, interfered with our best mislaid plans. After Father's passing, after the memorial service in Ohio, after Charlie and I flew to Michigan several months later to celebrate Mother's eightieth birthday, we returned home to L.A. in time for Charlie to start his next movie and die on location. Any haggling over where to bury Father was shelved. Literally, I see.

Father would laugh, not care one way or the other over where he'd end up, but me, I slip on jeans, t-shirt and sweater, my eye on the brass box, the size of a shoebox, crammed between *Grey's Anatomy* and a box of Tide. I reach up and grasp its smooth unadorned bronze, feel the heat of what was once his life beating back at my fingers, like a moth in a bell jar seeking release.

Cradling the box under my arm, I walk up the basement stairs to the silent kitchen in my sister's sleeping household. I locate my purse and the keys to the rental car and slip out the front door into the green Spring early morning, the shapes of rose bushes and irises lining the porch and drive, my heart thumping fast.

I step into the rental Ford Escort, the automatic opener making a ting-ting in the dawn stillness, and place the box on the passenger seat next to me. Absurdly, I consider strapping the box in but instead reach for my own safety belt.

It crosses my mind, the thought of dying in a fiery collision on a Michigan highway in May or encountering a deer hunter with a gun rack catching a whiff of my California liberal. I could get lost and never find my way back to the "blue" enclave of Ann Arbor, a stranger in my own America, my rental car a GPS dot on highways cutting through a landscape of fading strip malls and auto plants.

The Barnes farm looms large with a ferocious vibrancy, the faded red barn awash in yellow light. Uncle Martin uses it now for his collection of junked cars and motor boats but I grasp a memory of what once was: The tall windmill pumping water with the taste of iron sulfate, the scent of oats, apples and earth. I see Grandpa in his overalls walking with head thrust forward. I hear Grandma calling the cats to supper.

I pull up to the gate off Highway 2, turn off the engine, and step out to stand at the fence. No one is here. The house and barn are as abandoned as the rusted vehicles sprawled before them; the grass is a parking lot saturated in engine oil.

Not here. I couldn't possibly spread his ashes here.

I drive on to the town cemetery and walk around the tombstones of Barnes ancestors going back to the Civil War. I pass an inscription carved into marble:

> *Death is a debt to nature due*
> *Which I have paid and so must you.*

I hear Father's soft laughter. He was of them but not one of them.

Not the cemetery either.

In the final week of his life at a hospital in Cleveland, as he slipped in and out of consciousness, unable or unwilling to eat as cancer took its final hold, Father spoke of needing his passport, of crossing borders: *Raul Castro — we'll check on that in Honduras — vamos a verlos — we'll find that in Havana.* I knew nothing of his association with Raul Castro or of his dealings in Honduras or any number of other secrets about his life, but when he said *Lago Tarapoto* I understood.

Lago Tarapoto near the Amazon border area between Colombia and Brazil had been touted as an exotic and magical place where visitors could swim with the pink dolphins. This place of real legend had stuck in Father's imagination and he had wanted to take his family there, but Mother objected to flying in a single prop plane, plus there was the not-so minor detail of rebel soldiers infiltrating the area. Decades later, as I stood beside Father in the final hours of his life and he spoke of needing his passport to see the pink dolphins of *Lago Tarapoto*, I wanted more than ever to have gone there with him.

My cellphone is buzzing and because I'm certain it's either Mother or Rosie I answer without checking and snarl, "Yeah, I'm on my way back."

"Mira, como está?"

A lightness of being rushes into this damp lonely place.

"Alejandro, I can't believe you're calling me now."

"And why is that, mi Mira? Por qué no ahora?"

I strain to hear his voice above the rush of highway traffic, this voice that lured me down the racing railcars and river rapids of San Cipriano, and suddenly I have but one image in my brain, and that is of this beautiful man stretched out naked before me like a veritable feast. I recall how the hair on his chest curls down toward his loins, his lips, those arched feet, the curve of his neck, the skin of his hips, his wrists, the blue veins pumping his blood and the hardness of him when I touch him. I'm done with recollection. *Here and now* is what I want.

Again my phone is vibrating and I look to see whose calling. MOTHER it says.

"I miss you," I say, ignoring MOTHER, "I've been around too much estrogen lately."

"You need *testosterone,*" Alejandro growls his caricature of the cliché Latin lover and I laugh in a high-strung way and still my phone vibrates, a shrill demand. I tell Alejandro I'm coming soon, possibly very soon. He is surprised, encouraging, when I say I will make flight reservations and text him the details.

After signing off I am stunned for a moment by how I have acted on pure instinct, and when my phone finally stops vibrating I know it means Mother is either leaving a message or calling Michigan State Police to search for the body of her missing daughter.

—◦—

"I don't plan on leaving anytime soon but that's what Grace Kelly thought and look what happened to her."

"I wish you'd told me you were going out shopping," Rosie says, "I needed you around to keep Mom company."

"I can do that in L.A. I practically live with her, you know."

It's after dinner, Jonathan having been put to bed after drifting off in front of the Tigers game with Dad. It's just us girls now, a scary prospect, the Barnes sisters alone together in the kitchen, Margaret teetering about in the living room, and all three of us finishing the wine we've already drunk too much of.

I fret over how I'll break the news of my plan to go to Colombia. As impetus I have stopped downtown and bought a pair of jungle boots at the Military Surplus store. I think of saying gracias to Alejandro for giving me a reason to escape and gracias for providing a place to escape to.

The notion of telling Rosie I'm leaving seems even more daunting now that I've been anointed as Mother's official caregiver.

"It's just that I can't trust her to be alone with Jonathan," Rosie is saying, "You remember how when he was little Mother became fixated with the Deadly Nightshade —"

"Yes, I know —" I've heard this story a dozen times but Rosie forges ahead.

"— she found behind our house and took Jonathan on walks to see it. Can you imagine? Telling a two year old 'don't eat that flower it could kill you.' Talk about power of suggestion!"

"What are you girls saying about me?"

Mother is standing in the doorway, cane in one hand, a photo album in the other, having quietly materialized.

Not skipping a beat Rosie says, "We were discussing what a weirdo you are, Mother."

"Oh. Well. Tell me something I don't know."

Margaret drops the album onto the chopping block. Wine glasses rattle. Unusually teetery tonight, she resents having to use the cane Rosie's given her and so she flings it to the floor after it gets her to where she's going. Someone will always pick it up, and it won't be her. The cane falls — slam! — and I pick it up again.

"Look what we have here," Mother says of the album, "It's pictures of my 80th birthday party!"

"Mom," I say, "Why don't you hang the cane on something or lean it against the table? You don't have to throw it on the floor."

"Good lord am I really over eighty?" Margaret says, ignoring me, "I should check out now before I'm too old to do it myself."

"Sure, Mom, that's what we want," says Rosie, "Go stand under an icicle."

"Icicle? What are you talking about?"

"You told us if we stand under an icicle it could fall and stab us in the brain," I say.

"It's been known to happen," says Margaret.

"I made that album for you, Mother," Rosie says, "You were supposed to take it back with you."

Margaret pauses at the first picture of herself before an "80"-shaped candle on a frosted cake.

"Hey, I look pretty good here," she says.

"You look fabulous," I agree, and she does. Dressed in a blue Calvin Klein dress we'd found at T.J. Maxx, she is slim and bright eyed, although not smiling. Margaret rarely smiles in pictures. Fools smile; interesting people do not.

Rosie pours boiling water into a teapot. I recall the build-up, replete with arguments, to Margaret's party in Ann Arbor two years ago, before the down spiral; before Charlie's end and Mother's move west. Everyone met Charlie for the first time, he charming all with stories about moviemaking, his daredevil stunt tales mystifying Margaret, who couldn't believe someone could engage in such life-threatening antics.

"Look, here's Charlie," Mother says, as if he's standing in the room. I lean forward to gaze down at his laughing eyes; rugged, grizzled, funny Charlie lifting five year-old Jonathan in the air. Margaret turns the pages, pauses at the pictures of herself with friends; with her grandson; with Rosie; with Johan; with Jonathan again; with former neighbors and a few old college friends. Her predictably negative running commentary is relentlessly depressing (*"Oh, Molly's dead now. Karen died of multiple sclerosis, remember? Why was Jerry invited, he was always such an old bore…"*), and as I look at the pictures I become increasingly aware of an absence. Someone who was at the party yet somehow isn't present in this entire album: Me.

There must be a mistake, I think. I am nowhere, not in one instance, not even a group shot. I recall many people taking pictures – Johan, Rosie, even a professional photographer friend of theirs – and I remember some of the shots: Charlie and I in the hammock, me lighting the "80" candle, mugging with Jonathan, tiredly sitting beside Mother with cats on our laps. But there's no record of me having been there.

I look up at Rosie and am about to ask why she didn't include any pictures of me, but she's already slipping out the kitchen door, tea cup in hand, with an "I'm beat, good-night, all," as if the very consideration of my exclusion were inconsequential. From the hallway I hear her voice calling back, "Careful on the stairs, Mother."

Margaret doesn't acknowledge the warning, she's too wrapped up in the pictures, but I respond with a "sleep well," me the chump, a sap struggling to curry favor with my sister by pretending to not be stunned, by actually *accepting it.*

"She treats me like I'm two," Mother says, not looking up, "Oh, now look at Marty, he was a dear man, too bad his wife was such a pill."

"I'm not in any of these," I say, "Did you notice?"

"What? No, of course you are." It doesn't seem to occur to Mother that she's paged through the entire album without seeing a single picture of me. "You were there!"

"I know I was there. But there's no picture of me anywhere."

I'm irritated by my indignation. It's like I'm tattling to Mom, *see Mommy how mean my little sister is to me?*

"You must be in here!"

"Where am I?"

We page back to the beginning and look carefully this time, but there's not one shot of the birthday girl's other daughter. Could Rosie have deliberately neglected to include me in this album, or was it merely an oversight? Which would be worse: To be purposely ignored out of spite or jealousy? Or to be simply forgotten, as if my presence at our mother's eightieth birthday party were unimportant, both to Rosie and to Mother herself? I am surprised at how deeply the shock of hurt has cut me, and then by my creeping fury.

"You're right," Margaret concludes, "Well Mira, what did you do?"

"What do you mean what did I do?"

"You must have done something. And you know if Rosie's unhappy, nobody's happy."

It's true. Rosie invariably has a fierce justification for her anger and can be counted on to punish the culprit.

"Well?" Mother persists, "Did something happen during the party? Did you do something to upset her?"

"You're right, I must have done something," I say, "Said something."

And then I remember: Rosie claimed at the time that I'd been neglecting them. With Charlie's encouragement I'd been pulling free of the prevalent arguments, weary of the argumentative triangle and problems that were part and parcel of being with my mother and sister. Like Father had done when he married Gloria, I was eager to get on with my new life with Charlie, and so my trips east had dwindled, and I'd recently traveled west, choosing to visit the widowed Gloria on the Big Island of Hawaii. I had even taken to calling Gloria "the mother I didn't expect," for she'd become, if not like a mother to me, then certainly a dear friend, and this too rankled Rosie. Then, irked over some forgettable quibble during Mother's birthday party, I had turned to Charlie and said, "I wish I wasn't here," and Rosie had overheard. I apologized, pleaded exhaustion, jet lag, overwork dressing a film set the week before, but the truth had been spoken and there was no changing it. I really hadn't wanted to be there. And so now Rosie had gotten back. *Back at ya, sis'.*

Absorbed in her birthday album, Mother now merrily says, "When you figure out your offense, let me know." And feigning indifference, more shaken than I care to admit, I kiss my mother on the cheek, a sort-of good-bye kiss.

My thoughts turn to how I will pack the jungle boots and Father's ashes into my carry-on bag.

Back in my guest room with the smelly cat litter, I feel no guilt for my refusal to uphold my end of what Rosie infuriatingly requires of me, which is to be Mother's escort, to be rendered sexless and invisible, to be relegated to the role of spinster aunt, sister, daughter. What I want instead is to be a woman running away to her Colombian lover.

I'm going to have sex again with a man if it kills me.

I pull out my iPhone, make the reservation and buy the ticket to Cali by way of Miami. I send Alejandro my flight information.

How easy was that? *Thank god for the internet*.

Freedom with the tap of a finger.

"Come back alive."

*I*t's a stealthy departure in the pre dawn hours, the taxi arriving by prearrangement a block away, its engine running, the call from the cab company a vibration on my phone.

I am a thief — *no, rescuer* — of my father's ashes, transferred into a plastic CVS bag, the bronze box left behind on the shelf next to the Tide. Inside the carry-on I've wedged the plastic bag of ashes beside the boots made for sloughing through Amazonian jungle.

I slip down the front staircase, past the porch swing. Pale peonies stand sentinel in in the semi-dark and it seems even the flowers disapprove of the big red "A" for Alejandro I have branded on my heart.

The cab driver greets me and puts my bag in the trunk. I step into the warmth of the taxi. Soon we are pulling away from my sister's neighborhood, the massive green trees of Ann Arbor. The Midwestern landscape whizzes by in a whoosh of American cars on early commute.

At Detroit's Metro Airport I join the long security lines, my canvas bag innocuously rolling beside me with its harmless contents: A summer dress, t-shirts, cargo pants, and oh, yes, my father, or rather the remains of him. It is all so *light*, my traveling home-for-now. The toiletries in the ziplock bag are removed and placed in the bin on the conveyor. With the exception of the fluttering thudding beat inside my chest I am unencumbered.

Amazingly, I pass through security without a hitch. No one stops me, no one inquires about Father's ashes. Perhaps on the scanner they look like a giant tub of talcum powder, and besides, no one brings powdery substances *into* Colombia.

Once we are boarded onto the 7:30 flight to Miami I check my phone message from Alejandro just to confirm he awaits me.

> *Yo to espero, mi Mira.*
> *Tu amor, Alejandro*

Tu amor. I don't think of where I am, which is sitting in a steel tube preparing to take off into the sky.

We sit for twenty minutes, then another twenty. Finally the pilot informs us there's a problem with fuel, or lack thereof.

"We've got to drill baby drill," says the hefty woman seated beside me, "Or we won't have enough to fly our planes!"

When she heaves herself up to rummage through the overhead bin I get a good look at the large "Juicy" inscribed across her pink-velour buttocks. A tanker truck pulls up beside the aircraft. It's nice to know *someone* thought of fueling up before we puttered over Lake Michigan.

I take out my phone again and notice Rosie's message. It's eight in the morning, yet she's already discovered I'm out of her sphere of influence. Wistfully recalling the olden days of life without satellite communication, I press reply. Rosie answers on the first ring.

"Where *are* you? What happened to you, Mira? Did you just *leave*?"

This is a voice similar to our mother's but it emanates from a younger and stronger voice box. Here she comes, another mother for me, she who gains greater strength and fury as our mother's power diminishes.

"I'm not there. Just like you so beautifully pictured it."

"You just left! Jonathan is heartbroken!"

"*Jonathan* is heartbroken? You made me disappear from Mom's party," I say, "Like I was dead or something, like Mom's birthday was a wake for her other daughter who wasn't even there!"

It hasn't dawned on me until now, why my elimination from the album has so wrecked and infuriated me. My sister had in essence whacked me out of existence. I've become *anonymously extinct*.

"You left with Charlie to go back to L.A.! There weren't any good pictures of you!"

"Oh *bullshit!* You were just punishing me!"

Juicy Lady gives me a smirk of acknowledgement as in, *you tell 'em sister*. The aircraft is bustling with people moving about the cabin and I'm only vaguely aware of anyone in my immediate vicinity being entertained by my side of the conversation. From the other end of the line I hear a repetitive *boing-boing-boing*.

"Jonathan, stop —" *Boing-boing-boing.* "*Please*, Jonathan, no pogo stick in the house!"

I hear our mother shouting in the background, "Is she alright?" There is a slamming of screen door, the shrill barking of Benji. Rosie lowers her voice.

"Mira, I think something's wrong with Mom. Her balance — she's different."

The tanker pulls away from the jet; we're preparing for take-off. The flight attendants tell us to turn off all electronic devices.

"Look," I say, determined to get in one more salvo before we fall into Lake Michigan, "I can't fix what's wrong between you and our mother. I don't have a child, I'm not a mother, I don't know what it's like. But don't you see you're becoming just like her? You've become so fucking paranoid about your precious miracle child!"

"Do not curse at me, and don't you dare say I'm like Mom."

"Fine, but whatever problems you need to fix with Mom *you* have to do on your own." I'm speaking in a rapid-fire blur of words. The flight attendant walks by and gives me the stink eye but I keep talking. "We always said Mom loved you best," I add, "So now it's your turn to try and be nice to her."

"So you're just high-tailing it back to *Hollywood*." Rosie's scorn slides into the word and I'm tempted to remind her Hollywood isn't where I live.

"No. I'm flying to Cali to see Alejandro."

I love dropping this little bomb. I might as well say I'm flying to Mars.

"Oh, *come on* Mira, you have *got* to be kidding me! Aren't you too old for this?"

"No! I'm not too old! Speak for yourself, why don't you."

Juicy Lady laughs. The harried flight attendant leans into my face and says in no uncertain terms it's time to turn off my cell, and while I nod and say "yes, okay," the only person I hear is my sister.

"You're making a fool of yourself," Rosie asserts, the doc writing my life's prognosis. "You're going to fly all the way to Cali and see how different it is from when we were kids and then he's not going to want you."

"How do you know? What are you trying to say?"

Rosie's silence has me filling in the blanks: *You're past your prime. You're no longer desirable. And because you aren't desired you can't possibly be loved.*

"You know," Rosie manages at last to say, and I hear pity dripping like poison in my ear, "You don't need to act so desperate. I mean, look. I agree. You need to get over it. But not this way!"

My seatmate is elbowing me, pointing out the flight attendant who's made an about face in the aisle and is heading back my way.

"Get over it? Get over *it*? You mean Charlie? That *it*?" I try to catch my breath but it's strangled and constricted in my throat. "You know, you're right. I do need to get over *it*. And I know exactly how."

Brimming with righteous indignation, it seems a good time for me to disconnect and when I do I honestly wonder if I will ever hear my sister's voice again. I switch to airplane mode before the looming flight attendant can brand me a cellphone terrorist, slip the phone into my pocket and mutter a "sorry."

"Your sister," says Juicy Lady with a gleam of understanding.

"How did you know?"

"Only sisters talk to each other like that."

— —

"Don't ask an old woman to feed your cats.
They'll end up starving to death if she drops dead."

— —

Miami Airport is big, bright, modern and noisy, with shops and consumer distractions everywhere and me with hours to kill and in plenty need of distraction before my flight leaves for Cali.

At the duty free store I purchase Chanel facial products I wouldn't ordinarily buy and a bottle of Martel for Alejandro even though my last recollection of his drinking brandy was of him mixing it with Coke inside a *bota* at the *Plaza de Toros*.

A wavering reflection in a Ralph Lauren store window of some crazy women who happens to be me gives way to the display of a white linen sheath that is so elegant and lovely I know that, should I wear it, I wouldn't be crazy at all. *This is the me I could be.* I could be the me I could be arriving at Alfonso Bonilla Aragon International Airport, I could be the me I could be sipping a pisco sour on the balcony of a *finca* overlooking the rolling pasturelands of Cali countryside.

The linen dress turns out to be the cost of my monthly mortgage, but I buy it anyway and wear it out of the store, my jeans and t-shirt shed like old snakeskin and stuffed into the Ralph Lauren bag. It occurs to me I've fiscally lost my mind but it's refreshing not to care. I'm an irresponsible consumer and bad-bad-bad but it feels good-good-good, and who knows? This could be the last hour of my life before boarding a flight that crashes into the Caribbean. Holding that thought, I spot a Polo safari jacket in another section of the window display and re-enter to credit myself even deeper into debt. It seems reasonable to buy it since the jacket matches the military surplus jungle boots I'll be wearing when, in an image of another me I could be, I'll be trekking through emerald forests to the pink dolphins of *Lago Tarapoto*.

More spending impulses, even the purchase of fruit, scone and black coffee at Starbucks — *bad, swilling caffeine before a flight* — are delicious acts of defiance. *This is me, the nervous rabbit, running away to Colombia, going broke shopping in Miami Airport.* I settle into a seat with a view of the Tarmac to await the call to my gate and decide to call Dr. I, a merely preemptive act since I'm strangely not the least bit panicked, only panicked about being panicked.

"Mira, you're doing just fine," says Dr. I, "Have a wonderful vacation with your new boyfriend."

This is his way of encouraging me to have sex until I'm blue in the face, and while I once resented the insinuation that the source of my panic attacks may be partially attributed to sexual repression, I am today in full support of the current diagnosis and prescription, which is to screw myself into blissful oblivion.

I wolf down a Starbucks scone as though it was my last meal and think, *has a scone ever been this tasty?* I shake off crumbs, remember to cross my legs now that I'm wearing a dress, my new linen Lauren dress. I feel my pelvis shifting, my sexuality roaring like a river. I call my gynecologist office and am told the BRCA blood test results aren't in yet but I'll be notified as soon as they are.

I make the next call to my neighbor Juanita and in her gravely old lady voice she assures me she will feed my cats for another week. Then she laughs and says "You go, girl," this centenarian rebel who was eleven in 1925, roaring her way into the Twenties.

Morbidly aware of having entrusted a one hundred year-old woman to feed my cats, I call Magill, just in case.

Something is wrong, he is telling me, but I can't hear his muffled warnings between the loud garbled *"flight to Sao Paulo"* and *"flight to Buenos Aires,"* catching but snatches of *"our payment check — the Newport wedding — Cayman Islands account —"* and hearing only what I want to hear, which is that Jorge will check on Juanita and the cats.

"Flight 43 to Bogota is now boarding at Gate 5."

I tell Magill I'll be back in a week but I don't know this for certain. I sign off and hand my boarding ticket to the flight attendant with dark shining hair. She smiles, and when she speaks, I at first don't understand.

"Upgraded," she repeats. Her skin is flawless, dazzling stones grace her lobes.

"You perhaps have an admirer," she says before turning to the next passenger.

Another flight attendant tells me to turn left into first class. I am stunned, utterly shocked, by the roomy plush seats, the little tables between them, the offer by yet another flight attendant to hang my jacket. I struggle to adopt a nonchalance I do not feel and I'm glad for the linen sheath I've impulsively decided to purchase and wear.

I'm offered champagne. A hot towel for my hands. A bag with toiletries rests on the little table beside my seat. There can be no other explanation for this other than Alejandro.

Settled into my spacious seat, the champagne a soothing effervescence lighting up my bloodstream, I check my messages:

Bienvenidos, mi linda Mira. I will see you soon.

We take off and lift up over the white city of Miami.

Maybe it's the champagne, the Antigua coffee, the new dress and first class seat and destination into a lover's arms, but should I go down into the Caribbean I will do it with a full buoyancy and lightness of spirit. I hear that clichéd old song in my head but hell it's true: *On a clear day you can see forever.*

The world is vast and beautiful and boldly clear and as we jet to the blue horizon I think, *what makes me so special that it would be my plane that crashes?*

Maybe I'll just be one of the millions of ordinary rest of us who end up alive at our destination.

Amazonia Victoriana

— ~

"It is every mother's nightmare to outlive her children."

— ~

This is the forest of ages, a deep teaming primeval land stretching below as we descend, its mass of green giving way to the distinction of colors and trees. It is the Colombia I saw in a dream only it wasn't a dream but a place I once knew.

Peru's communist military junta had driven American businesses along with our family out of Lima, and when we relocated to our new home in Cali we had to fly into Colombia's *Valle del Cauca* despite reports of a jet crashing into the side of one of the nine thousand foot mountains surrounding the airport. Our arrival in Colombia entailed no conscious awareness of the brilliant greens or sweeping grasslands and sparking rivers in the verdant valley below, but rather was superseded by the presence of Mother gripping the airline seat and softly weeping in terror. That was when Father said, "You don't get headaches, Margaret; you only give them."

Decades later, I understand how Mother's fear blinded me to the beauty below, but this doesn't stop me from pressing my lucky chrysoprase crystal over my heart that is galloping at triple speed as the jet descends and touches down onto the tarmac of Alfonso Bonilla Aragon International Airport.

— ~

"When you get into a vehicle with a shovel
in the trunk be aware -
Someone might use it to bury you alive."

I am not expecting a reunion with the Colombia I knew as a teenager, and yet crossing the threshold into the jetway's permeable tube instantly transports me to the Cali of my youth. International airports are regulated environments — temperature, security and crowds are managed and controlled — but jetways are another story. The caressing warmth and humidity, the sultry seduction of a certain sweetness in the air, this has not been altered by either global warming or even the entire reconstruction of the landscape. I am back in the land Father brought us to all those decades ago, dressed in my Polo safari jacket with no clue as to what lies ahead.

The airport itself, however, with its cold air, commercial perfume and stale coffee scents, is innocuous. I get through customs and walk among other international flyers arriving and hurrying to catch flights.

I pass beautiful Latin women in summer finery, men in business suits. My legs feel light, eager to walk after thirteen hours of airport layovers and flying. After customs I join the swirl of the crowd joining at the vortex of baggage claim where I have no baggage to claim, only Alejandro.

I see him from a distance before he sees me. He is pacing, hunched forward, talking into his cellphone, and the very sight of the entire package — the lithe walk and thick dark curls at the back of his neck — catches the breath in my throat.

He turns and sees me, says something into his phone, switches it off. I dodge a rouged matron, a young couple kissing over a spray of roses. Alejandro awaits my approach, regarding me with a dominant look, and just as I begin to wonder why I find the murderous look on his face so sensual, he breaks into a roguish smile. There is no doubt as to why I am here and I don't care how obvious it is to relish being so thoroughly assessed and undressed. He comes up to me, takes the handle of my bag in his grip and kisses me. His other hand encircles something around my wrist and when we part I look down and see I am wearing a bracelet, a band of gold with a row of brilliant cut emeralds.

"What is this?"

"It is for you. Do you remember?"

"Remember — ?"

"Come." He is guiding me toward the exit. "You have no more luggage?"

"No," I say, then recall what I'm supposed to know about this familiar golden bangle with its row of emeralds.

"Your mother," I say, "She wore this!"

"You admired it, and if my mother were here she would want you to have it."

"Oh, Alejandro, it's too beautiful, you must have someone, a niece —"

"I have no family now." He says this with cool finality. "It is for you."

"Then thank-you. I love it."

He enwraps my neck into the hook of his arm and draws me in and whispers into my ear, "Now I want to see only this on you."

"*Only* this?"

We are outside in the lush warm air of the beautiful tropical Colombia I thought I would never see again, and only now do I realize how I loved it here more than any country we lived in. I feel the contrast against my skin, the difference between this rain-drenched nation and drought-tolerant California.

Alejandro lifts my bag into the back of a black Range Rover. I see garden implements, the tools he uses for work. Only for a second do I experience a twinge of anxiety, remembering Margaret's macabre remark about shovels in trunks, when Alejandro pulls me into him in the parking garage and gives me a kiss that is a promise to continue what was left unfinished in Venice, and somewhere in that kiss I forget what Mother said.

"Be aware that in a foreign country where you don't know the customs you could say or do something that could turn a friend into an enemy."

The drive from the airport in Palmira toward Cali is a blur in the long evening twilight. I take in views of the sugarcane plantations stretching out toward the Cordillera Occidental and Central mountain ranges then glance down at the exquisite emeralds sparking from the gold encircling my wrist. Released from airport control, I am ecstatic with scents and sensations — the sweet floral air, the sultry tropical wind buffeting the open spaces of Alejandro's rugged Range Rover.

"So beautiful," I say, resting my head back on the seat, succumbing to the menagerie of perfumed scents. Banana blossoms? Frangipani?

"It is ginger," Alejandro says. "There is a ginger farm nearby."

"I can't believe I'm here," I say.

Airports and travel have made me dull and it's a rare moment of feeling no anxiety, the anxiety having been replaced with pure, unmitigated desire. I think of the alternative to this moment, awakening in Rosie's house, facing another fractious day navigating the mood swings of my mother and sister. I'm free of all that.

"Much of this land used to be wild and beautiful," Alejandro is saying, "But we make sacrifices for progress, do we not?"

There's a bitter edge to his tour guide spiel when he tells me of the environmental destruction of his country's forests, how in the name of progress the region is being destroyed at a certain number of hectares per year, and how at this rate it will all be gone in four decades.

"But this is not what you want to hear, mi tourista Mira. You have come to see los delfines rosados de Amazonia and you will see them, I promise you, even if you are the last American to see them."

"Environmental groups all over the world are lobbying to stop deforestation," I say.

"It is an endless cycle," he says, looking forward to the highway cutting through long industrialized stretches of sugarcane fields and vast expanses of other crops, "There is much poverty here."

Is he condescending or explaining? I know about the poverty in his country, it is in my country too.

"Many people here wish to join the global economy," he continues, "but to do this they must sell the natural resources. They do not care as long as they can put food on the table. And many times the people are manipulated by big businesses. Colombian businesses yes, but also Americans who do not live here but come in and rape the country until there will be no land for our people to live in. My countrymen will have big box stores and wide screen televisions so they can watch the rich in your country dress up and quarrel with one another and then wish they can be like them."

It's an old argument, one I heard back in the seventies when my father was one of those Americans presumably raping the land, and it has been complicated since by Colombia's drug wars, paramilitary forces, and political duplicity by its own government. I want to say, *sure, blame everything on the Americans*, but keep silent. I want to argue with Alejandro as we once did, but remember a not inconsiderable detail which looms large: His wife Maria was murdered by paramilitary thugs, he himself was held prisoner by rebels when he was barely out of childhood, his father was shot, his friends have been killed. If Alejandro wants to lecture, let him.

We drive into the city of my dreams in this Valley of the Cauca, and at this moment Alejandro almost achieves the impossible, the time transport I have wished for, simply by driving us by *Iglesia de le Ermita* and its landmark gothic spire, lit-up bright white and ornate on the skyline overlooking the city. What washes over me when I see it is the memory of Father and me walking alongside *Rio Cali* that runs through the city and its park, the mutual thrill we felt on the night when Americans and Colombians gathered together in the Colombo Americano building to watch on television U.S. astronauts first stepping onto the moon. *Los Estados Unidas Llegan a la Luna!* The Colombian papers cheered. We were gods then, and my father was a good American.

Alejandro pulls over suddenly into a parking space at the park.

"It feels strange, does it not?"

"So you know," I say. Of all the countries loved and left behind, this one was the last and hardest to leave.

"Come," he says. He steps out of the Rover then he's at the passenger door gripping my hand. I step down and he's lifting me up off my feet and carrying me in his arms.

"What? Alejandro, where —"

And then I get it and laugh. He's carrying me through the olive grove like before and it's all so hauntingly the same, the twisted trunks and feathery leaved branches bowing like giants harking our passage in a fairy tale, we the possessed, the aged children. He sets me down against the trunk of one such giant that may very well have been here *then*. He gives me a kiss as soft as a boy's then steps back and peers off into the night as if looking for someone or something.

"One more memory trip?" says he.

"Why not," I reply.

We walk fast toward wherever he has in mind, some other memory. The night is on the heels of twilight, in the footsteps of people leaving work for drinks, at the fringes of the park, the lights in the cafes. The scent of saucy garlic and rice emanates from restaurants on the square. Salsa music calls from open doorways and here we are, walking on a street I feel deep in my bones but really don't remember, not really.

"This is so familiar," I say. Alejandro leads me to the door of a large international hotel. *Oh,* I say, *Oh yes.*

"*Yes?*"

White marble and an air of washed surfaces, too many waiters, piped music that ran on the same loop, big Americans and rich Europeans in the bright efficient dining room. But there was one spot that seemed a haven, a dark bar to the right of the lobby, and Alejandro is leading me to it now and here we are, in the same bar, and it seems almost criminal that this bar could still be here and not my father.

"This is where I first met you," I say, "We were new to Cali, staying at this hotel before we found a house. You and your parents met us here for drinks." *And I wanted you the moment I saw you.*

Low round tables, a hushed darkness, just as hotel bars are supposed to be, where women look beautiful and men in suits light their cigarettes. This is where my mother smoked and flashed her cocktail rings and our parents talked business or tales of travel while we kids, Rosie, Alejandro and I, dared each other to eat the unusual crudités served in bowls like peanuts that turned out to be roasted ants covered in chocolate.

"You and your sister walked in with your parents, and you were wearing a pink dress."

"God, that pink dress. I was miserable. I missed my friends in Lima, we were living in a hotel —"

"But I made things better, no?"

"Oh, you made things better," I say. I reach out to touch his face and for a brief instant he flinches. I am surprised by how hot his skin feels.

"You were not what I expected. You said you were a Marxist. A Norte Americana Marxist in a pink tutu!"

"And you were crazy for Led Zeppelin."

Alejandro orders champagne Kirs. The serving staff is indigenous, near invisible in their uniforms, and I recall how hard it had been to get used to this and I never did, though some American kids took to it easily, ordering cokes at the country club, signing their room numbers. It was easy to pretend you're an adult or become an Ugly American when cowed people were always waiting on you.

"What do you remember of my father?"

I ask this because in this plush shadowy little hotel bar I seize fleeting impressions of the man who was Harry Barnes. While Mother is as bright and clear as the rings she wore on her fingers, Father was a mystery, a whiff of soft laughter. His was the hand that lit the cigarettes and paid the checks, and amidst all that talk, so many people talking, he was but one of the few who was really listening.

Alejandro caresses the back of my hand on the champagne glass.

"A good man," he says, looking down, not into my eyes but at my hand, the glass of bubbly, "You father at first seemed like all the others — big, jovial, soft in the belly —"

"— like other American fat cats."

"— but he was different. He wasn't an imperialista."

"I once heard a rumor Father arranged the ransom to free you. Father didn't go into the jungle and personally deliver it, did he?"

Alejandro looks toward the bar where a group of men in sleek shiny suits congregate.

"No, it was his associate. A younger man, the swimmer — I saw him give el comandante a duffle, then he was gone and later I was delivered to a place and allowed to go free. Papa was a wealthy man but he didn't have that kind of money."

"So my father —"

Alejandro's mouth on mine isn't so much a kiss as a move to silence me, a warning that I stop talking. When his lips pull back he looks over my shoulder, his hand gripping the back of my hair in a manner that is authoritative and surprisingly, unexpectedly seductive.

"Do not speak of this now," he says.

"Of course," I whisper and look into his eyes. He shakes his head but slightly.

"Este es nuestro momento," he says, "Ahora, aqui."

This is our moment. Now, here.

He places money on the table and grasps my wrist over the gold and emerald bracelet. His grip is so tight I wince from the pain and start to pull away but he is standing now, pulling me toward him, talking quickly, quietly.

"We will go to my *finca* now where I have prepared *ceviche* for us and to-morrow we will play tourist. That is —" his voice teases suddenly as though the warning of a moment ago never happened, "— unless you wish to go dancing now. Do you remember *la cumbia*?"

"Take me to your *finca*." I say.

— —

> *"If you think people are conspiring against you, you're probably right."*

Vegetative darkness swallows me up as we ascend the long drive through the hulking shapes of banana trees and thickets of ochre bamboo to Alejandro's *Hacienda Vista de Lejos*. Again the scent of flowers. *Guabos churimos* he softly says, seducing me with the syllabic sound. *Guabos churimos*. But then I hear Alejandro's sudden tense exhale of a curse beneath his breath.

A dark SUV awaits at the drive, and emerging from the back patio's rounded arches are the shapes of two men. One inhales a cigarette to a hot ember glow.

Alejandro briefly grasps my left wrist.

"Say nothing to Mauricio about the bracelet."

He then releases me to turn off the engine.

"No Spanish either," he adds, "It's better that he thinks you forgot it."

"I did forget a lot of it," I say.

I feel a jolt in the back of the vehicle when he retrieves my bag, the slam of the back trunk as he turns his attention to what I can only surmise are his unexpected and unwanted guests.

"Que tal, Mauricio?" Alejandro is saying, his tone coolly offhand.

I open the passenger door and slip out, landing on soft damp soil.

"Estamos en el vecindario," says the bigger man of the two, Mauricio I assume. I have a faint recollection of that day in Newport Beach, a face behind the windshield of the lead Mercedes in the cavalcade that appeared more funereal than celebratory. Alejandro is by my side, his arm around my shoulder, nudging me forward while at the same time keeping me close.

"Mauricio, allow me to introduce to you mi linda Mira. Mira, this is my friend and brother Mauricio Corrida."

"Con mucho gusto," Mauricio says, holding out his hand. He is an imposing man, in his early sixties. His face is shadowed and the very politeness of his voice belies a hard distrust.

"Nice to meet you," I reply in English. Mauricio's handshake is a swift nicety and the man with him makes no move to introduce himself. The night air is thick with cloying menace but my instinct is to pretend to be at ease, to be distinctly American, or rather distinctly Midwestern American.

"Alejandro has told me so much about you," I blurt, realizing the instant I say it how guileless this sounds.

"Has he?" Mauricio turns to Alejandro and if I could see in the dark I would hope for the hint of a fraternal smile.

"I mean, your wedding. Congratulations. Feliz – feliz –" I pause. No Spanish.

"Felicitaciones," Alejandro says, condescendingly coaching me to speak the traditional word I already know. I feel his thumb digging into my shoulder.

"Si," I say, awkwardly, la gringa idiota.

"Your bride Isabella is beautiful, you are a lucky man," I say with the distinct apprehension that such complimentary platitudes are being misconstrued as too personal.

"Yes, she is a lucky woman too," Mauricio says, having the audacity to compliment himself. I instantly know I dislike him at the very moment he is inviting us to join them for dinner and dancing back at his estate.

I turn to Alejandro with a *no, no please* in my eyes but Alejandro is looking at Mauricio and not shaking his head or begging off with the justifiable excuse I would hope for, but rather pausing, considering, as Mauricio speaks forcefully to him in Spanish. I discern only a few phrases in Mauricio and Alejandro's rapid fire exchange: Mauricio announces a change of plans, Alejandro indicates it's a bad time for such a change, but the certainty and finality of Mauricio's argument accelerates — I catch *en contacto con alguien* — until Alejandro reluctantly concedes, turns his back to Mauricio and faces me. The darkness makes it near impossible to read Alejandro's face but his intonation is amazingly blasé, casual, and this is what he passes off to the men who flank him.

"A minor business matter tonight," Alejandro tells me, "But you will enjoy the hospitality of Mauricio's family, which is renowned. Isabella has asked about you."

He's doing the big sell and I try to buy it.

"I'm sorry," I say, "aren't we —" I want to say *don't we have a say in this?* Instead I laugh. "No comprendo," I say in my worst gringo Spanish.

This seems to crack up the other man, the one accompanying Mauricio. "Tenemos una discoteca," Mauricio says to Alejandro, then he turns to me, "We will have dancing and dinner, you cannot refuse."

"But your house," I say to Alejandro, "Don't I get a tour?"

"Mañana," the other man with the cigarette says and grins, a silver-toothed flash of friendly persuasion. He's a small man, this other one, shorter than me. Irrationally, I think *I could take him on.* This seems like a ridiculous thing to be considering, and in confirmation of the absurdity of it I'm suddenly aware of standing in the dark in a remote suburb of Cali with three Colombian men, one with a shark's silvery grin, the other appearing to have some persuasive power over Alejandro who is the third man, the one who my libido has chosen to blindly, passionately trust.

"Bueno," Alejandro says. He tosses my bag back into the SUV without a second's pause. The movement is final and resolute; there is no anger but rather resignation over this so-called business meeting that apparently can't wait.

Alejandro opens the passenger door. I look at him and debate the wisdom of refusing to get in. *I have to pee* is what I want to say. *Can't I at least use your bathroom?* But the other men are standing nearby waiting and I sense that my willingness to do what Alejandro wants me to do is part of some test and that if I resist my fate will be controlled by someone other than Alejandro, and I don't want it to be these men.

"I seriously hope I can remember how to *cumbia*," I say, as if this were the most important thing on my mind.

Mauricio looks at Alejandro. Alejandro says quickly, "I will refresh your memory, Mira mia" and I say, "Okay" in a sing-song way, grinning like an idiot.

Alejandro is behind the wheel, starting the engine, turning away from his home in a roundabout move which positions us in front of Mauricio and the other man, the driver, in the SUV. A flash of headlights moves over us and in that brief instant I see Alejandro's face. He is grim, haggard, suddenly older. Following behind us, the SUV's headlights shine onto the backs of our heads. I am certain we are being observed, and as he drives I wait for Alejandro to speak but he doesn't. He is thinking and driving. He drives away from *Hacienda Vista de Lejos* while looking back in his rearview mirror at the contours of his house, the silhouettes of banana fronds.

"What's going on?"

"Laugh," Alejandro says, "Look like we are flirting."

I perform for our observers behind the headlights on the road behind us. They don't hear the strangled quality of my laughter, nor do they see me reach for Alejandro's hand on the stick shift.

"Good," he says when I lean across and kiss him softly on the side of his mouth. He faces forward and drives. "Ah, Mira, I am sorry."

"I'm scared." I whisper, then for our audience I lick his ear, smile and nuzzle. He laughs.

"You are fine. You will like Mauricio's *finca*," he says. "Very luxurious, you will see. He is an excellent host."

"And you — he — have some business tonight?"

"Yes."

I can see his knuckles protruding hard and boney as he grips the wheel. I feel his heartbeat pounding against my lips on his neck.

"More rose bushes to landscape in the coffee orchard?" I say.

"Perhaps. You will be fine," he says again, as if trying to convince himself.

I lean my head sideways upon his shoulder, an awkward move across the gap between passenger seat and driver. This is for more than show although despite fear, maybe in addition to fear, I still desire him. He'd spoken that day on Venice Beach of wanting to disappear, and all I could think of was not losing him.

"Are you in trouble?" I ask.

"You must trust me," he says, "Can you do that, Mira?"

He has told me to stick to the instructed script, although I have no lines, certainly not in Spanish. I must wait, not ask questions, pay attention, feign ignorance and say nothing about the bracelet.

"Do I have a choice?"

— —

"Stay away from people with guns. Period."

Mauricio's sprawling compound in the affluent Versailles neighborhood is the size of a small housing development. There is Mauricio and Isabella's mansion, then Josephina's house further on down the way, plus servants' quarters and stables, and even a *discoteca* blasting *vallenatos* from somewhere 'round the bend behind the papaya grove. The place is ablaze with festive lights emanating from crystalline chandeliers hanging in the giant *ceiba* trees. There are splashing water gardens landscaped into what I recognize to be Alejandro's distinctive style — a garden of unbridled beauty and refinement. Sweeping views overlook the valley and the glittering city of Cali below.

Isabella welcomes me with an effusive hug, her doe eyes teary, as if we are longtime friends instead of client and garden designer who met but once to set-up her wedding party decor. Her sisters-in-law, Mauricio's sisters, are simultaneously cordial and chilly. They shake my hand in the customary way of some Colombian women by laying a hand in mine, and while this is supposed to seem lady-like and feminine, it feels more to me like grasping a cold dead fish. The eldest, Josephina, winces and withdraws her delicately manicured fingertips from my violent American handshake while the other sister, Bonita, who's possibly around my age, introduces me to her full grown sons and Mauricio's sons from a former marriage, their names whizzing by — Eduardo and Eduardo, Felipe, Manuelo, Esteban — and they in turn introduce their girlfriends and friends, young people from the *Universidad*. Everyone is beautifully dressed in designer jeans and ironed shirts or elegant lacy tops or cottony summer dresses.

Outdoor spaces lead through jungle pathways where *palmas de cera* explode skyward and exotically striped bromeliads line the path. I see Alejandro's landscaping hand here, his contrasting colors of deep burgundy foliage and emerald ground cover, and then we're moving through patios with sprawling bougainvillea, gliding into open seating areas with elegant cushioned furniture. I can't get a fix on the mansion but sense that it's as big as a hotel, a compound of stonework and arches, balconies and patios in which exteriors blend into interiors and chandeliers are present fixtures indoors and out. A long banquet table has been set with *empanadas*, tropical fruits, layers of flower arrangements and frothy puddings and cheeses.

The air is tropical, languid; a breeze drifts across a sparkling pool where guests mingle and swim. Alejandro stands on the other side of this pool with Mauricio's business associates, a few men in dark suits who glance over at Alejandro's *novia nueva* but don't care to be introduced. Alejandro appears to be arguing with them in a quiet, controlled fashion about something other than designing Mauricio's gardens.

Isabella suggests that I "visit the loo," having learned her English from British schools in Spain, and draws me into the pool house where I can "refresh and change," as she puts it. I set my bag down in a beautiful private bathroom suite where my roller bag has been placed on a low table beside my "Polo" shopping bag.

There is an impression of any hold I may have on control being gently removed, such as my suitcase having been brought here without my knowledge. I wonder if it's been searched, if some suspicious soul has found my father's ashes. After Isabella leaves I zip open my roller, inspect the contents; all are here, including Father, who is more of a talisman to me at this moment than the chrysoprase crystal necklace I unhook from my neck and place on the tile counter.

Finally, I relieve myself into the toilet next to the bidet. The bathroom fixtures are golden, the tile iridescent. I slip out of my dress and underwear and try to remove the bejeweled bracelet Alejandro has given me before stepping into the shower but it refuses to unlock. So I pretend I'm posing in a *Vogue* perfume ad and bathe in emeralds and try to relax.

Showered, scented and creamed with *Maja* bath products, I emerge from the pool house wearing the emerald bracelet I am not supposed to say anything about. I've slipped back into the white linen sheath. Underneath I wear a fresh lacey thong that I hope will be part an exclusive showing later tonight.

Throbbing *vallenato* music draws me out to the maze of patios under the trees. Groups have gathered according to gender. The cousins, Mauricio's sons and nephews, talk loudly over the dj's combination of salsa and modern mixes.

"Ella es guapa, si, pero es lenta —"

"Tienes que practicar."

Their laughter is raucous and I gather they're talking about women, rating their performance or appearances in some way. I hear phrases that would attest to a certain lewd rating system — *she's fast on the trigger* — *runs hot* — interspersed with moments of intensely opinionated remarks in rapid fire Spanish I can barely understand. And then I do understand, the words drifting my way with sharp unwanted clarity:

"You can't miss when you stick it in the ear."

They aren't talking about women. They are talking about guns. And killing.

I hear it so clearly and bilingually I truly don't know if it was said in English or the Spanish I'm not supposed to know.

The man who is Mauricio's driver gives me a rakish smile and calls out, *"quieres bailar, Mira Gringa?"* The young men turn to politely acknowledge me, but it's the driver, three times their age, who leers. Little Big Man on campus. I smile and continue walking without projecting even a hint of understanding. Never would I have thought I'd want to be middle-aged invisible, but this is my most fervent wish now. The man's grin widens to laughter at what appears to be his own private joke.

The women are seated in one of the many patios and I can't get to them fast enough. On the way I search the pool area for Alejandro but don't see him anywhere.

"Mira, you are looking so fresh and lovely!" Isabella says with her bright beautiful smile. From their perch around a coffee table her sisters-in-law give me the up and down overview.

"That is Ralph Lauren 'Blue Label,'" Josephina says with begrudging approval, "I saw it on InStyle."

She is a beautiful aged woman with creamy bleached skin, blackened hair and a subtle nip/tucked jaw. Her black eyeliner is back in fashion but I suspect she has been wearing it since high school. I want to compliment the long pink and white sleeveless dress she wears and hesitate before I go ahead and do so, her reaction confirming what I anticipated. She shrugs as if I'm attempting to curry favor.

Isabella launches into a nervous monologue about having been color-matched by a stylist, and I'm eager to oblige her with my interest. Am I a Spring? A Winter? I haven't the foggiest. Josephine and Bonita exchange bored glances. I suspect Isabella is starved for girly conversation. Or friendly conversation. This may be a den of bitterness, but I can't forget that the sisters are but two left from a trio that once included Maria, Alejandro's murdered former wife.

Isabella jumps up to escort me to the banquet table, where she discourses on the art of making empanadas and her love of pudding. She's trying hard, but this effervescently youthful bride is but one breath away from bursting into tears. She laughs, she gestures emphatically; she admires my bracelet.

"Mauricio always brings me jewels after his disappearances," Isabella says, "If I ever choose to run away I will have quite a collection of emeralds and diamonds!"

"Disappearances?"

"This was also before we married, so I cannot complain."

White bird in a golden cage.

Suddenly I spot Alejandro coming out of another building, flanked by serious men in casual summer suits. He catches my eye from across the reflecting pool lights and heads around the pool toward me. He nods to Isabella, looks to me.

"Alejandro," I start to say, but he stops me with a shake of his head, a glance elsewhere.

"Lovely Mira," Alejandro says, and absently takes my hand. "Quieres bailar?"

Isabel smiles at us, the lovebirds, as he leads me away to the *discoteque*.

"We have to go," I say, "This place — I'm sorry, Isabella's nice, but I'm really freaking out here. That guy over there was talking about shooting someone in the ear."

"Velasco? Si, yo se. He's a blowhard. Ignore him."

"How can I — ?"

Alejandro interrupts me with a loud, phony laugh. He crushes my head against his shoulder, the move basically saying *shut up.* We are not alone and there are others around us, the Eduardos, the girlfriends. Electronic salsa pulsates like no salsa I remember. Alejandro twirls me away, dances a few steps, then pulls me back into him and whispers in my ear.

"Laugh for me, Mira," he says.

I see Mauricio watching us, raising his glass in a facsimile of affable toast. Flummoxed, I laugh on cue and execute a salsa move I can barely remember.

"I like the way you move in that dress," Alejandro says.

He pulls me back into him and to the thrumming of the bass our hips float in tandem. Mauricio lurks like a jealous lover and it occurs to me that someone is always trying to separate us: The FARC back when we teenagers, Mother just weeks ago, and now Mauricio. A surge of dogged willfulness overtakes my unease. Never do I feel more rational, more certain of what I want. The rhythm of the music overtakes me and I choose to help Alejandro by doing his bidding — by dancing, by laughing.

Alejandro kisses the sharp licorice of *aquardiente* off my lips and I move my breasts against the hard heat of his body and smell the honey spice of the *guabos churimos* on the evening breeze.

Mauricio doesn't dance. He lights a cigar, or rather, has his cigar lit for him. He watches Alejandro. Isabella twirls across the dance floor, a delicate mistress of ceremonies. This celebration under the chandeliers is to honor Estefan who has graduated from a *universidad* in Bogota, but there is something else afoot here, something forbidden and secret. I overhear someone jokingly add that Esteban will soon be studying "submarine biology" in La Jolla — near San Diego, California, that is.

We conjoin at the patio by the pool where Mauricio and the sisters and Mauricio's ubiquitous driver await our return. Josephina and Bonita fan themselves with their gossip magazines, lean their heads together in whispered conference. I am aware of the sheen of moisture on my arms, how by every appearance I am the lascivious *gringa*, their sister Maria's would-be replacement. Alejandro has encouraged me to be a spectacle, the dancing *gringa imperialista,* and while I'm aware of the sisters' dislike I also sense this is intended as distraction on Alejandro's part, that I am part of some plan of which I have yet to be informed.

"Tengo que hablar contigo," Mauricio says to Alejandro. It is a command. Alejandro shrugs, turns to me.

"This orchid is native to the Cauca Valley," he says casually, reaching to a bloom overhead, "*Cattleya candida.*"

"When are we going back to your house?" I ask.

"Después, vamanos," Mauricio says. He has walked up the path where he stands at an archway. Alejandro gives me a small smile and steps back.

"We must stay here tonight," he says and kisses me on the cheek like a brother or friend. He glances back toward Mauricio, who waits at the arch, and in an instant I am frightened for him.

"Isabella will take care of you. Hasta mañana, mi bella Mira."

"You're — ?" But I stop myself from saying what he sees in my eyes, which is: "You're not staying with me tonight?"

I sense the others watching us; Mauricio's sisters sip their evening café as they pretend to look away. Alejandro senses my humiliation at having been abandoned. It was never my intention to fly here to visit these people. Alejandro's silent unspoken answer to my question is an amused downward turn of his mouth in mock *pobresita*.

"Keep the orchid for me, Mira, I will be back for it in the morning."

I say nothing and take the waxy blossom and hold it to my nose, but it has no scent. As Alejandro walks away I recognize his jaunty step as feigned.

Isabella steps out of the circle of the others, her face a study in guarded sympathy as she offers to show me to my guest quarters.

"You will love it," Isabella says of the 'Cielo Suite.'

I doubt it. How can I love the prospect of sleeping alone in the home of Mauricio Corrida? All I can hope for is a lock on the door.

— ⁓

"Always first check the sheets of a strange bed before getting in.
There could be spiders or worse inside."

Again my belongings have been moved by mysterious hands, this time into the opulent Cielo Suite. Everything about me has been taken over. My luggage. My clothes. The jeans and t-shirt I'd stuffed into the Polo bag before the flight, even my socks, have been washed and dried and neatly folded and placed atop my Patagonia roller.

"Ah, good, Sesi has cleaned your clothes," Isabella says, "You travel light!"

I survey the dresser table top with its silver decanter and bathroom sundries, the blue satin linens on the king sized bed, the gold-filigreed full-length mirrors.

"Your home is just beautiful and you are a wonderful hostess," I say.

"But," Isabella rejoins with a smile and pauses.

"But?"

"But you would rather be at Alejandro's."

"Am I that obvious?"

Now that I've been prodded into inadvertently, rudely, conceded my wish not to be here, I backtrack, "But you've been so gracious and kind, and you've made me feel so welcome."

"It is challenging to be here sometimes," Isabella says, her voice wavering slightly, "I did not know how challenging it would be. But I do love Colombia. I had better," she laughs, "It is my home now!"

"How did you meet Mauricio?" I ask, wondering if I really want the answer, but she appears so lonely, so eager to talk and, tired as I am, it's the least I can do.

"Oh, I met him at a party near the embassy in Madrid, I was a translator there. He was so charming, and divorced, which is good. Though many Latin men have mistresses, that is not for me. He spoiled me terribly, flew me here first class —"

This is sounding terribly familiar.

"— and I never went home."

"Never?"

"Except on my honeymoon, of course. *Our* honeymoon. Mauricio — he works very hard to make life good for all of us. So he is gone a great deal. But I have company here. Josephina and Bonita. And Sesi."

I hope Sesi is not the man who likes to "stick it in the ear."

"I am sorry my husband is so businesslike. I promise you will get to see more of Alejandro soon."

"Is Mauricio planning more landscaping?"

"No, not at all, not here, no!" Isabella's laughter is nervous and I feel sorry for her. How can a bird in a golden cage grow to maturity when its wings have been clipped?

"Mauricio and Alejandro are clearly close friends," I nudge.

"Oh yes, when you think of what they have been through together."

"Mauricio's sister Maria —"

"Yes, of course Maria, bless her, I wish I could have known her. But, no, I mean when something like that happens to you when you are young, it changes everything."

"Yes?"

"Mauricio was there with *las Fuerzas*. They were there for each other."

"Yes, I see," I say, although I don't see.

"Chained together onto a tree —"

Oh?

"— and for months. Wasn't it months?"

"Over a month, almost two," I say, although I don't exactly know. This is news to me. Alejandro and Mauricio chained together?

"Mauricio joined *las Fuerzas* but he was so young. To be chained in that way, together, it changed them, and they are brothers since that time."

"But they aren't with FARC now," I prompt.

"Certainly no," Isabella says, "But I have tired you with my talk! And after your long travels! You must sleep, and you will see, soon you will have Alejandro to yourself and Mauricio will stop being such a big brother."

Big brother in arms.

"Goodnight, Isabella, and thank-you again."

"Oh, I am happy for the company and someone to talk to!"

In the bathroom I slip out of my dress, wash my face, my arms. I still can't get the bracelet off and wonder if I'll be able to sleep with it on or if I'll be able to sleep period. A white cotton robe has been folded next to the towels and I decide to put it on and wander around the room in an effort at convincing myself I'm fine, just fine, really fine.

But I'm on the verge of a panic attack, the first one in weeks, and all I can do is employ the usual tricks, the controlled breathing, the isometric tensing and releasing of muscles. I slide open the glass doors leading onto the balcony and feel the breeze and listen to the distant music and muffled voices. The trick at this point is to be outward, not inward. My heart will speed faster if I listen to it, but I don't listen to it. Instead I listen to the world outside my heart, the rustling of the yellow sugarcane and the *igua* stirring the leaves of the *palma de cera* until finally I am lulled into the dark vegetative tranquility. The panic attack is over, over, over I repeat like a mantra, it is gone, gone, gone. At least for tonight.

*"First nights in strange places invite trouble.
Always lock your door and windows too."*

* * *

"Bㅤut you see, I have Harry Barnes' daughter."
ㅤAlejandro speaks in a voice so low I mistake it at first for dreaming.

Tropical night air suspends me from deeper sleep and I am afloat and adrift on this large flat bed under a cool blue layer of sheets, waiting for Alejandro who does not come.

"And what do you propose to do with her?"

"The usual, my friend. The usual."

This is no dream. This is Mauricio and Alejandro talking in the silence of the night somewhere on the patio not far enough from my window. Any doubts as to my retention of Spanish are decidedly gone; I understand every word.

I don't move. The swish of a sheet, the intake of breath before I stifle it, these they might hear. I listen to the tinkle of cocktail ice being dropped into crystal glasses, the shuffling of feet at the patio table. It's all terribly Bond-James-Bond, I think, the cocktails, the ice, the men's voices, and it seems amazing to me they don't suspect I could hear. Then again, the men may not know my guest room is situated in full-fledged orchestral seat proximity to their conversation.

"You know we analyze the phone logs looking for snitches. We have an insider at Telecon. Your messages to Harry Barnes' daughter —"

"You have spied on me."

"Your timing with her is either terrible or brilliant."

"It could buy us some cooperation until it's done."

"And then you will be done with her?"

"Perhaps."

"You are an ordinary man. Is that what you are saying?"

"What do you think I am saying?"

"I think you are not so ordinary. Not at all."

"Then you have your answer. I must tell you the garden looks good," Alejandro adds, changing the subject, it seems.

"That is Isabella's category. And yours. Your landscapes are always yours. I would know your gardens anywhere, especialmente por aqui."

"Por aqui, si." There is resignation in Alejandro's voice, or is it simply exhaustion?

"I know you don't like this, Alejandro, but sometimes we do what we must and not what is legal."

"Después, bien." Alejandro speaks with a snap of impatience and soon they are joined by another man who I recognize from his tone as the leering amused driver, Velasco.

"Yo necessito ir contigo. Para tu seguridad."

"No."

"Si. Es final."

Their voices bleed into the crunch of footsteps as they recede further on down the path and then they are gone to another part of the estate where they will scheme and talk about how Harry Barnes' daughter *will buy cooperation until it's done.*

First, I get up and check the lock on the balcony door. Not that it will make any difference but it will at least buy me time to fall apart. To cry and rage and panic and feel sick, only I do none of these things. Even when he appears to have some plan for me, even when Mauricio expects me to be part of this *final,* whatever this *final* is, I still hope to trust Alejandro.

What could these so-called businessmen, this cartel, possibly want from me? I'm not rich, not politically tied certainly. There is nothing of significance to my being Harry Barnes' daughter and even so, my father died some years ago.

What could they want from a dead man's daughter?

I dig into the black hole that is my bag in search of my phone and feel a make-up compact, a tin case of Altoids. I frantically dump the contents onto the bed but my cell doesn't come spilling out among the Kleenex and antibacterial lotion and cosmetics. Did I leave it in the pool house? On the plane? When did I last have it? *Has it been removed?* I search in the bathroom, in my suitcase, in the pockets of the safari jacket, but it is gone.

Stolen, usurped, my communication with the outside world. Terror is what I feel, sudden, uncontrollable terror, but I must tamp it down, not let it get the better of me. My iPhone is an extension of me, it has my life, my apps, appointments and contacts and phone numbers, even those damnable emails from my sister. If someone has taken it, that someone plans to listen to it for "snitches." Either that or it's a simple theft of opportunity, as they call it; perhaps one of the cousins or their university friends took it.

Quickly, I pack what little I have unpacked: toiletries, the dress. It remains dark out and I don't know where Alejandro is or if I should dare to trust him to get me out of this when clearly he's gotten me in. I curl up into a fetal position on the bed. Fetal is good, fetal is for thinking, or maybe not thinking, maybe just reviewing how it got to this and what my instincts tell me.

I pull at the bracelet I can't slip out of. It feels like handcuffs.

I stay in this fetal position in my thin little nightie for the remainder of what's left of darkness — an hour, two — not moving, listening to the *Valle de Cauca* as it awakens, the exotic call of foreign birds, the whole damn infuriating terrible and seductive land.

The sky turns magenta like the grim aftermath of a bloody battle, and with its color I become aware of the sound of the steady civilized clip-clip-clip of cutting shears. It is a common occurrence on estates such as this -- the arrival of gardeners quietly pruning in the early morning hours. Unless you live in Southern California, where by contrast they come to noisily mow and blow. Get me home to the mower blowers, I think. Forget the Amazon, forget the pink dolphins; just get me out of this place.

The clipping sounds move to beneath my window, and my hope is that they are the work of Alejandro. Not Alejandro the man who brought me to this place but Alejandro the boy who hiked with me through the luminous meadows of his beautiful country, who doused me in waterfalls and pressed me down upon the warm rocks of swimming holes, the boy who rubbed my feet in the sun and kissed all of me with his tongue and read me Pablo Neruda's love poetry.

> *...I love your feet*
> *only because they walked*
> *upon the earth and upon*
> *the wind and upon the waters*
> *until they found me.*

Sixteen years old, and even then Alejandro knew how to romance a woman.

I rise and go to the balcony and yes, there he is. The gardener. Lady Mira's lover. Who last night stood her up in favor of some nefarious interaction with a sinister Cali businessman who most decidedly does not have Lady Mira's best interests at heart. Who maybe stole her phone.

I search for a clue to this man in the way he tends the garden, how the muscles move against the cloth at the shoulders of his shirt, the way he hunches down and studies a clipping before discarding or keeping it. He drags along two small canvas bags, intent on separating one cutting from the other, placing a stem piece in this bag, a root or bud in the other. His concentration is so complete it's hard to believe he spent the night plotting my fate. From my vantage on the balcony I watch the power of his haunches as he bends and straightens, the stretch of his arms and length of his fingers, and it is infuriating that even still, after what I know or don't know and must know and don't want to know, I want to trade places with the petals he touches.

I step back from the balcony railing and onto a leaf which crunches beneath my bare foot. He looks up, sees me, and walks toward the balcony until he is just below, and then he shifts his gaze down to my feet and then up though the folds of my nightgown.

"Buenos dias, Señorita," he drawls in imitation of an old Hollywood movie Mexican. His smile is that of a rake and I am a flower oozing sweet. I believe he can smell my panic like a dog, but to me he is more like a jungle cat. Cats wait quietly and patiently for their prey. I don't smile back nor acknowledge his humor but rather look down upon him and let the breeze catch the hem of my nightgown. Yeah, smell the prey.

"Where is my phone?" I say.

I register the sudden watchful look on his face and it occurs to me he might not know. His eyes say, *careful* but he laughs and shrugs as if it doesn't matter. But it matters. *We analyze the phone logs looking for snitches,* Mauricio had said.

I turn back into the room and leave him below. I check the lock again and shower quickly, this time with no interest in the lovely bath amenities. I dress in the jeans the silent minions had cleaned last night. I slip on a silky green blouse that's wrinkled yet stylish and besides, it's important that I wear my colors, that I look as beautiful as I possibly can so that I may use whatever hold I have on Alejandro, even if it is only our lost youth. I must hold onto the belief that those you love when young remain loyal no matter what has come since.

There's no denying I trusted him because he was the boy who once read me Neruda. Or maybe I was simply in love with Neruda.

...we have grown together
but we did not know it.

When we were young betrayal fell within the jurisdiction of the larger world. It was the world our parents made, not ours. That innocent place we created, the land of Neruda, is what I came to Colombia for, only I'd be fooling myself if I said I came here only to recapture lost youth. If that was all I came here for I would have given up on Alejandro the instant I heard, *"Yo tengo Harry Barnes' daughter."*

"Don't meddle in other people's politics or you'll find yourself wearing a "corbata" just like the rest of them."

One of the cousins, the one with the slicked back hair, is arguing with Mauricio's sisters at the breakfast table while their brother quietly eats his eggs with perfect precision, cutting across the yellow eyed yolks and shoveling the *patatas* onto the top of his fork. Josephina is countering the cousin's argument by dropping inflammatory remarks about *Los Estados Unidos,* and so I raise a questioning eyebrow to Mauricio. He gives me a sympathetic grin, and I get the impression he knows I understand them, although per Alejandro's instructions to me I don't let on. What the cousin is talking about is social media and the new political movement in Chile and how a young woman revolutionary is changing the way they do politics and the old ways of Che are over.

Josephina on the other hand counters that the *Norte Americanos* are at fault for everything that is wrong with Colombia, and while the cousin doesn't disagree, his major slant seems to be us-the-young against you-the-old, as in old-fashioned Che and way-old Castro.

I notice how the young cousin — Felipe — talks of *revolucion* even as he issues orders to the servants whom he barely acknowledges.

"Quero hamon," Felipe says to the man serving his eggs, and the man disappears into the kitchen.

My father may have been an *imperialista Americano* but he knew how to say *por favor* and *gracias* and ask about the welfare of those who worked for him and appreciate what they did. He may have ascribed at one time to the domino theory on communism but he was not of the one percent, un-like the self-satisfied people at the breakfast table this morning, who are clearly Colombia's one percent, the landed gentry.

"There can be neither amnesty nor impunity for crimes against humanity," Josephena says.

"She speaks of your country." Mauricio is amused. He pats his mouth with the white table napkin, sips his coffee, clears his throat. Everyone at the table falls silent. The cousin especially shuts up. His uncle is the big man; to respect him is to fear.

"My country? Oh, yes, I understood," I say, *"Los Estados Unidos."*

Josephina snorts in derision. The cousin gives me a flirtatious wink. It was right to wear the green silk blouse, I think. It's part of the costume. The *Americana* on holiday.

"My sister is saying," Mauricio continues, "That the Americans' war on drugs finances the paramilitary which kill our people."

"Not me!" I say, *"I* don't condone that."

"It is ironic, don't you think, America's appetite for drugs? They blame us, when all we do is sell them what they want."

"But," I flounder, *how naïve am I supposed to pretend to be?* "You export coffee. That's *my* only addiction."

The cousin's laughter is suddenly explosive. Josephina cracks a smile.

"Yes, we have a lucrative coffee route," Mauricio says in all seriousness.

"Ella es bonita pero un poquito estupida," says the cousin. Mauricio watches me carefully. And now I know for certain what Alejandro has all but told me, and that is that Mauricio is Cali Cartel, or what is left of it — *we have a lucrative coffee route* — and my presence in his home is both a coup and threatening to him because he suspects I have *some* power, *some* influence when in fact I have nothing of the kind.

And now the man of the house launches into a languid, insulting monologue about how everything is the fault of my country: the paramilitaries (our government funds them!), the drug trade (*we're* the consumers). He speaks of the displacement of indigenous peoples in a campaign of counterinsurgency known as "take the water away from the fish," the water being the civilian population, the fish the FARC. I want to say that the counterinsurgency has worked, that it's forcing the FARC into peace talks. But I sense this hypocritical thug has a vested interest in keeping his country in a constant state of civil war and that *his* interest is in bullying and subjecting anyone to his will.

"You Americans are too puritan," Felipe the cousin says.

"Oh, but you don't know the half of it," I say to diffuse the political charge in the room, "Alejandro has made me a convert. For Alejandro I am ready to join *la revolución* against my Puritanism."

Josephina and Bonita visibly recoil, but the men are amused and diverted, as was my intention. When in doubt, revert to your inappropriate *gringa* sexuality. I may be the naïve American here among the coca growers in the Valle de Cauca but I am still *la rubia que todos quieren* — or rather the blonde that used to be wanted, when I was a quarter century younger.

Isabella is suddenly present, laughing at my innuendo, hugging Mauricio good morning, pouring her husband more coffee. When I agree to another cup of "Mira's favorite drug," it seems I can almost convince myself this is a comfortable breakfast conversation among friendly hosts.

"Is that Alejandro?" Isabella says.

Alejandro passes by the window carrying his canvas bags of clippings. He looks like one of the staff, but Bonita interjects.

"What is he doing?"

"He's pruning," I say.

"Mira, tell him to come in and eat," Bonita says, "We have gardeners to do that."

"He *is* a gardener."

"He is an artist," Mauricio says.

I slip through the sliding glass doors into the moist morning air. Alejandro sees me coming toward him and hoists the canvas bags onto his right shoulder.

"Alejandro, I want to go," I say.

"Yes. I understand."

The garden is less beautiful to me this morning. I am assaulted by scent, the dense overhead growth of guava and blood orange trees, the jasmine and *yarumos* cascading down. Fecund growth encroaches everywhere and I imagine the hallucinogenic *datura* spiraling northward into Norte America where we will be overtaken by our southern neighbors with their magical thinking and half century-long civil war.

"Where did you sleep last night?" I ask. Alejandro's linen pants are softened by wear and his hair is littered with bits of leaves.

"Here," he says, and gestures over to a chaise lounge by the pool, as if sleeping on it were the most logical thing.

"I want to go," I repeat, and try to keep my voice from rising hysterically, "I heard you scheming with Mauricio last night. I don't know what it means but I just want you to get me out of here."

"I have it."

He kisses my neck, whispers in my ear. His skin smells like flowers.

"What? What do you have?"

"Your phone. You must trust me."

"*You* took it? You keep asking me to trust you, Alejandro, but how can I trust you when you —"

"Please, Mira," he says and turning his back to the house, to the others watching us from inside their glassed-in breakfast nook, he points to a vine cluster of white bell shaped flowers.

"*Floripondio,*" he says. I don't want a botany lesson.

"Do you hear what I'm saying?" I'm nearing tears and it's all I can do to speak without screaming. "Please let's go. I've heard about enough about *imperialista Norte Americanos.*"

"Then you must help me," he says.

"I *have* been helping you. And I'm crazy to do it, to be here."

"We will go to *Lago Tarapoto,*" he says. "We will play at *touristas.*"

"Then get me out of this place."

"Bien. Be angry and loud about it."

"What?"

"For me. Demand that we go. Be la Norte Americana princesa. They expect it anyway. Be quick and pack your things. Be ready. Do what I say."

"Fine!" I shout, but this no performance. I am disgusted, shaking, caffeinated. My desire for him has been replaced by confusion and fury at Mauricio, the sisters, the cousins and sons and the leering Velasco, who is clearly an assassin or at best a gun fanatic. I see them watching us through the sliding glass doors' view to the patio — Isabella with her mouth in a wide "O" of surprise, Mauricio turning to stare.

"This isn't the vacation I came for," I shout with what is certainly sufficient outrage, "I want to see *your* home and garden. I want to see the Amazon!"

The cousin Felipe leans across the table to say something to Bonita and Josephina. Alejandro shifts the canvas bags and adopts the uncharacteristic expression of a man cowed by his demanding lover. I walk away from him and up the pathway toward the house, push through the doors into the breakfast room.

"Too much café Colombiana," I say, to the astonished diners and it's partly true. My heart is beating so fast I wonder if I can keep this up without blacking out.

"Oh, I am so sorry," Isabella says. The dear woman is indeed sorry. She wants so much to be a good hostess, to entertain her new *Norte Americana* friend.

Back in the guest suite, I'm glad for my foresight of having already packed my bags shortly after the discovery of my missing phone, the phone

Alejandro took at some point before my luggage was searched. I leave behind the duty free bottle of Martel with which I no longer wish to be encumbered, a gift for my scary hosts.

I step into the bathroom to gather my cosmetics and put on my chrysoprase necklace but the glint of aquamarine-colored crystal, my talisman and protector, isn't on the counter. It isn't on the dresser. The chrysoprase that keeps me calm, the chrysoprase that is *my magical thinking* is nowhere to be found. Standing in bare feet, debating, reviewing, I remember.

It's in the pool house.

Barefooted, I slip out into the hall. From the downstairs breakfast room I hear the commotion of Isabella's defensive cries, the cousin joking about how her poor hostessing is driving *la Americana* away. Isabella's voice rises. Josephina tells her to *calmate.*

The young newlywed's abrupt tears are a convenient distraction while I wander down the maze of hallways of this mission-style colonial, past open rooms, stucco archways and tangles of dense bougainvillea and intricately tiled corners spewing ornate little fountains. It is all so sprawling and huge that I'm overcome suddenly with the futility of my search for something as simple as an exit to the gardens.

At last I reach the pathway to the pool house and it takes me by a boy skimming the pool's glistening surface with a net. He notices me then looks away.

No one is in the pool house, but there are the towels and Maja soaps and other niceties, including robes and bathing caps. No sign of my chrysoprase. What did I expect, after all? Suddenly this whole trip, this entire visit, seems utterly foolish to me. *My protector, my beloved talisman,* nothing and no one can take the place of my magical crystal. Without it I can't face any of this, I can't possibly go to the Amazon. Without the chrysoprase my plane will crash, without it I will be kidnapped, beaten, murdered.

"Tu tienes que harcerlo…"

"Pero no con el!"

"Si con el. Es final."

Mauricio and Alejandro's voices echo through the pool house. I stand frozen, regretting my fleeting comprehension. The room's sharp echo and the deliberate careful words makes it easier for me to understand.

"Why don't you have Velasco give it to him?" This is Alejandro, associate of drug runners, who speaks..

"If Velasco's caught putting a plug in him it will be tied to me," says Mauricio.

"It might still be tied to you."

"Not if you are sightseeing in the Amazon with Harry Barnes' daughter."

"No puedo hacer todo que tu quieres," Alejandro says.

"Basta. Make it happen."

I hear Mauricio shout an order to the pool boy. The boy replies *la señora esta ahí* and I realize I've been caught. Caught listening to a conversation about someone *putting a plug in him.*

I walk out of the pool house doing my best to look like I haven't heard something I shouldn't. *Hear no evil.*

Alejandro looks me down and up, from my bare feet to what I hope is my clueless, innocent face, the one that has no inkling of their plan to *put a plug in him.*

"How long have you been posing there, my beauty?" Alejandro speaks to me in a tone of measured, threatening flirtation. I don't wait for either of them to answer his question.

"Someone has stolen my necklace!"

I nearly shout to keep my voice from shaking. The best defense is a good offense, I always say.

"Come, Mira, you misplaced it packing."

Alejandro's slow approach is gracefully restrained and tense. Like a shot he reaches out and grasps my arm. It appears to be a gentlemanly action, but his thumb digs into the back of my triceps and I almost cry out in pain. It is a warning.

"I have to find it! I can't travel without it." As soon as the words leave my mouth I realize how wrong they are.

"Then you will stay here," Alejandro says.

"No, absolutely not. I'm going to see the Amazon if it kills me."

"You were looking for it in the pool house?" He is patronizing to the little lady and her jewels.

"Yo pienso que ella entiende Español," Mauricio says after watching our little back and forth. He then turns to me. "Entiendes Español?"

I wait for a moment, then say, "Un poquito." Every gringo knows what "entiendes español" means.

Mauricio stares at me for a beat longer, then erupts into condescending laughter. I really have entertained him, me the gringa clown.

"You are touring this woman to Amazonia?" he says to Alejandro, then turns back to me. "Señora, you will need bug spray in the Amazon, not this silly necklace."

Mauricio pulls something out of his pants pocket, holds out his large hard fist, turns it over, opens his hand, and there it is. My chrysoprase, my life, in the palm of his dark meaty hand.

"Oh my God! Thank-you!" I gush, "Where was it?" I pretend gratitude when what I feel is repulsion and loathing. He tauntingly dangles the sea green crystal from its chain and when I reach out he pulls it back an inch, laughs, then hands it to me in a discarding gesture.

"The honest pool boy found it," says Mauricio, "You *Americanos* are too quick to accuse. We are not all the criminals you think we are."

"Thank-you, Mauricio, and thank-you to the pool boy, truly," I say with showy gratitude. I slip the necklace, *safe, keeping me safe,* over my head.

"And oh dear, did you say bug spray?" I continue, playing court jester to the hilt, "Well, I guess it's worth a few mosquito bites to see the pink dolphins!"

"You must take her to see the parrots," Mauricio says, "Or *las guaguas*" he adds, and laughs.

"Let us get your bag, Mira," Alejandro says, "I've made a reservation on an afternoon flight." He hasn't let go of my arm and his thumb threatens to mark out a bruise.

"What are the *guaguas*?" I ask, but Alejandro shakes his head and glances at Mauricio. The two men exchange a boyish smirk.

When we walk past the pool I shout out a *gracias* to the pool boy who gravely nods and continues trawling.

Josephina and Bonita appear relieved, suddenly friendly. Isabella by contrast is distraught. She wears a lacy white cover-up over her swimsuit, her legs tan and gorgeous, pedicured feet in gold Tory Burch sandals. I hear her say *claustrofóbico* — and Josephina retorts, *this is how we stay safe*, but this doesn't appease her, and then she is engulfed by Mauricio's arm on her shoulder.

My bag is here, having been mysteriously transported from my room. This is how it happens, everyone so kindly and courteously taking over until one loses control of one's own belongings, until one becomes a prisoner in this place.

"You must wear proper socks with those," Mauricio says, as I slip my bare feet into the jungle boots.

"You are so right," I say, sticking to script as babbling tourist. "I'm so excited to be seeing more of your country. Thank-you, thank-you so much, you have all been such wonderful hosts."

I take Isabella's hand, and when I see the sheen of sadness in her eyes I find myself wishing we could take her with us, free her from this compound of desultory days spent by the pool listening to privileged young people talk of *revolución* against their comfortable class.

Alejandro grasps the handle of my roller and hoists the ubiquitous canvas bags, the ones with the garden clippings, onto his shoulder. He also carries another bag, a small yet conspicuously elegant Louis Vuitton.

I hug Isabella, shake Mauricio's hand, nod my thanks to the sisters, who stand back watching, clearly eager to see my corrupting influence on their sister-in-law take its leave. We walk back toward where the cars are parked, down the graveled landscaped pathway, Alejandro close at my side. I turn back to see Isabella looking as though she's losing her best friend and am overcome with an impulse to assure her.

And so I say it without thinking.

"Hasta luego." In perfectly accented Spanish.

The air grows suddenly denser, thick with the humidity and perfume of hundreds of flowers within the encapsulating walls. Mauricio smiles knowingly, then nods to Velasco. We keep walking but the driver follows us down the path.

"Tu hablas español, Mira?" Velasco calls out to me.

"Hasta la vista baby," I reply in my best Arnold Schwarzenegger, this time laying on the gringo accent, but I am caught, guilty, and it shows on my face.

— ~

— ~ —

"If you can't think of anything nice to say

about someone

figure it's your instincts telling you

that person is trouble."

— ~ —

"No es importante," Alejandro says to me on the drive to the airport, "He had a pretty good idea you understood some Spanish."

I sit with my arms crossed in front of me but it is not from the cold. The air is languid and I'm grateful to at least be back in the Cali countryside instead of choked inside Mauricio's walled compound.

"I didn't like your landscape," I say by way of retort.

"Oh? And why not?"

"Too claustrophobic."

"Si, claustrofóbico," Alejandro says, and I recognize the word Isabella spoke to her sisters-in-law. How quickly one learns the language, I think, when living in it.

"My landscape had limitations," Alejandro explains, but he is not defensive.

"Oh you mean like gunmen, kidnappers and cartel guys? I can see how it can really crimp a designer's style."

Alejandro reacts with surprising calm.

"We will be alone now," he says.

"Big romance. Swatting mosquitoes the size of my purse in the Amazon jungle. Thanks but I'm going home."

Alejandro reaches across and puts his hand on mine.

"You are not going home. I am taking you to see los delfines rosados, just as you promised your father."

I pull my hand away.

"I hear you have Harry Barnes' daughter."

Alejandro glances up into the rear view mirror. I wait for him to explain himself, but he says nothing.

"I don't like wearing a bracelet I can't take off. It feels like handcuffs."

"I have the key," Alejandro says, "It will be all right. You will see."

Alejandro has lowered his voice, but I hear his words above the passing wind and engine roar.

"Why can't we go back to your house? Why are we going to the Amazon now?"

"Because we are escaping."

Again Alejandro looks into the rear view mirror.

"Maybe *you* are escaping, but I'm going home," I say, "I have a say in this."

"No."

"*NO?*"

"No you do not have a say. Many people don't have a say, and now you are one of them. People who are hungry all the time, who are powerless, people whose families are displaced, whose homes are raided and turned to dust. They have no say. Children who get no education, no chance for a better life. This happens in my country. It has turned to crap and corruption because people have no say. Now you will have no say."

He downshifts as we approach the highway. He turns to look at me and I see the eyes I remember, the conviction.

"Are you going to say 'you Americans' now?"

Alejandro accelerates onto the highway.

"I am not accusing you," he says. His voice softens. "I am saying you don't have a say about what happens now because it is you who has decided to love me, to come here and be with me. I didn't expect Mauricio to — to do what he is trying to do. He found out who you are. You did not have a say in that either."

The man is not accusing me of being a *capitalista Americana* but rather of loving him. I cannot refute that. It was never only about sex or romance when I decided to come back to his country.

"I have not told you everything," Alejandro continues, "because I needed you to have courage."

"You're asking me to be someone I'm not," I say.

"Then perhaps you don't know who you are."

It's almost laughable when Alejandro pulls out my phone with its pink "Hello Kitty" case given to me by Jonathan for Christmas. He keeps his eyes on the road, quickly punches in a number.

"Si. Si puedo a las cinco en el Parque Santander. Bien."

Alejandro finishes the call and slips the phone back into his pocket even as I reflexively reach out to take it.

"Not now," he says to me, "I need it, I will explain later."

"When? When will you explain?"

"We are being followed by Velasco. Don't turn around."

I sit rigidly in the seat. We pick up speed along the highway. I smell cattle farms and pastures; the wind whips my hair.

"That way is *Club Campestre*," Alejandro says, a non sequitur if I ever heard it. *Club Campestre*, where we stretched out by the children's splash pool after the children had gone, a hideaway for us to kiss under the sun, chlorinated water pouring off our skin, our hips hugging the warm tile under our white club towels.

"So many times there we almost lost our virginity together," he says, "but I always stopped and said you were too young. The greatest regret of my life!"

"This trip is the greatest regret of my life," I say.

"Ah, Mira, where's your sense of adventure?"

Alejandro pushes on the accelerator and we surge forward, fast.

"Is he still on our tail?"

"He is having fun with us. Don't look back. We will lose him eventually, I promise you, but it will take time."

"I'm not going to the Amazon."

"Mira, you must."

"Who are you planning on killing?"

Alejandro is silent. I watch him internally debate on what to say and deciding finally on nothing.

"I know what *sicario* means," I say. *Assassin. Hitman.* "Is that what you are?"

His expression is one of surprise; he is genuinely pained by my question.

"No. I am a gardener. I believe in life, not death."

"That's funny," I say, but neither one of us laughs. "And what about him?"

I look in the side mirror at the SUV riding up close, too close, and I can see in the driver's seat Velasco grinning wide at me like he's some big hungry vulture and I'm a piece of potential road kill.

"I'd suggest you not ask him that," Alejandro says, "For he would be delighted to tell you."

— —

"Don't get on an airplane without first saying a prayer."

When we park at Alfonso Bonilla International Airport, Velasco pulls his black SUV into the long-term parking space beside us, his smile wide and convivial.

"Ah, Senora, Amazonia!" he says to me, "You are to have the experience of a lifetime."

I'm not about to argue that any experience with this thug would indeed be the experience of a lifetime, maybe even the end of a lifetime. Near dizzy with panic, I grab hold of my roller and walk swiftly toward the terminal.

"I'm not going to *Amazonia*," I say, "I'm going to Los Estados Unidos."

"Pobrecito Alejandro," Velasco jeers.

We enter the dry airport air and I can't believe that less than twenty-four hours ago I landed here and now I'm leaving in a completely different frame of mind. Forget love. Forget romance. Just get me out.

I search for the American Airlines ticket counter but my urgency has rattled me and I'm engulfed in a crowd of hurried passengers, unable to see where I'm headed. I keep walking fast, the hard edges of the heavy jungle boots digging into my ankles. The men keep pace, Velasco looking across me at Alejandro. I feel them both assessing how to deal with me, flanking me. An armed soldier stands guard near the security check-in. Alejandro gently touches me, a delicate stroke moving down my free arm. I move my arm away.

"Ah, so then," Velasco says, "You are smart to leave Alejandro to his fate. He can no longer hide behind the big man's daughter, no?"

"Hide?" I say, pausing to get my bearings. I see signs for Aviana Airlines, Lan, TACA, Iberia, but no American Airlines.

"What happened in the forest must stay in the forest," Velasco says and turns to Alejandro. "Verdad?"

I look to Alejandro. "What's that supposed to mean?"

"It means nothing," Alejandro says, but he speaks too quickly and I suspect now what I feared all along, which is that by having me with him Alejandro is in some way protected, if only by a hair, and that by my leaving that protection is gone.

I look from one man to the other and notice that Velasco eyes dance with the cold proud thrill of his work. It doesn't matter that Mauricio is crazy. He is the man with the power, and thanks to something that happened a lifetime ago, *something that happened in the jungle that must stay in the jungle,* thanks to that, I am forever an emissary of my father's legacy.

"Come on," I say, "Who am I to Mauricio anyway? Is Mauricio crazy?"

"Please, Mira," Alejandro says. "I will speak alone with her," he says to Velasco.

"Es tu funeral," the *sicario* replies. He steps away from us but hovers close with studied nonchalance, glancing at the check-in counters, a group of smartly dressed flight attendants. His black leather jacket and dark shiny pants, lined face and hard scrabble hair, all scream out hard-ass, assassin, killer.

I take a breath, steal myself, and finally look at Alejandro. I don't know what I am expecting to see on is face — disappointment, anger, bitterness? — but what I see instead are eyes that shine a glowing fondness, a tenderness, upon me.

"This is goodbye forever," he says, and leans down to give me the gentlest of formal kisses upon my cheek, a noticeable reprisal of the past.

"I have to protect myself," I say, but there is no time to explain, to be defensive, to persuade him.

"I understand, Mira. Go."

"Can't you come with me?"

Alejandro shakes his head.

"Will you come visit?"

"No. I told you. This is goodbye forever."

"But I don't understand."

"No. You don't."

Because I want another kiss, a good one, not a formal one, I step closer to him. He steps back.

"Go," he says, his face hardening.

"I thought you wanted me to come with you, that you needed me."

"I cannot force you. Go."

Again I take a step toward him and again he backs away, and so I reach out, clutch his face in my hands, kiss those lips, feel his hands move reluctantly around me, pull me into him, his body desiring and simultaneously resisting then relinquishing. I hold on, won't let the kiss I can't get enough of end. This is supposed to be good-bye, but somehow it is not.

"Okay," I whisper, afraid suddenly of this new person I'm becoming; and from this new person comes the words, "I'm with you, I won't leave you."

Relief washes over Alejandro's face, and something else. He's proud, I realize, proud of me, but Velasco is suddenly beside us, grinning, acting for all the world like he's been invited along, a delighted third wheel forming our little *ménage a trois*.

"Parque National has many delights for the touristas, you will see," Velasco says, "The *guaguas* especially you will like."

"That is enough, Velasco," Alejandro says.

I don't ask what *guaguas* are, but if the man's sly leer is any indication, I suspect I won't like them at all.

"If you're in a bad situation, scream for help. Some people could have saved their own lives if only they had screamed."

"We're here, Father."

I'm not really talking to the remains of the man in my suitcase at my feet, and Father didn't really request that I scatter his ashes here, 'here' being the border town of Letitia on the banks of the Amazon at the conjunction of Colombia, Peru and Brazil. But for me it's the beginning of a silent promise to a man who as he lay dying uttered disjointed words about his passport and the pink dolphins of *Lago Tarapoto*.

Letitia is a pretty little town with pastel painted buildings, visitors, and the occasional armed soldier or guard, an ideal place for exchange of contraband. The air is hot and still and suffused with the sounds of birds screaming from the edge of the Amazon forest just across the way. We are in the lobby bar of the Decalodge Ticuna hotel where we've been given "complimentary welcome drinks" following check-in. The Amazon River — *the Amazon!* — is just across the road.

I am astonished by the sleek comfort of this hotel: the large and sparkling pool, the modern upholstery, the only nod to the jungle being the huge green and red sculpture of an anaconda suspended across the restaurant ceiling. I had expected something more rustic after our two-hour flight across the Andes from Bogota in a single prop plane, me seated between Alejandro and the ever-present Velasco, my so-called bodyguard, while grasping my chrysoprase over the course of the bumpy flight. You would think that a remote town five-hundred miles from a highway wouldn't have such sleek hotel furnishings and electronics shops and elegant sculptures in its parks, but then there's money here, quietly laundered money apparently, and both Alejandro and Velasco appear conspicuously at home.

"Your father, he was our enemy," Velasco is telling me, his imagination fueled by the *aguardiente* he breathes across the café table into my face. Alejandro sits beside me appearing by all who don't know him entirely impassive and bored. There's a calculated, mildly threatening 'Eurotrash' look to the dark stubble on Alejandro's face, the manner in which he slouches against the hard-backed chair and takes no interest in the conversation, if that's what you'd call the ongoing spew of hostility emanating from Velasco.

"The CIA, los Estados Unidos, they pay big money to fight los Americanos' addiction to drugs," Velasco says, "But the money is for death squads, do you know that?"

"I — don't know what to think," I say, pretending to be at least superficially polite. As long as we play at mock holiday, we are on holiday, *la tourista* visiting the lovely border town of Letitia where guns, cocaine and cash quietly exchange hands.

"Tu tienes que pensar, Señora. Pensar." He taps his head, draws out the last word.

I sip my beer. My armpits are damp with a combination sweat and Cristalle Chanel, which I've splashed liberally onto my neck, overuse be damned, and my feet are roasting in the jungle boots I feel entirely ridiculous wearing. I want to go to our room and get away from this vile asinine man, but Alejandro bides his time and appears to be waiting for something or someone, perhaps the someone he made the phone call to on my phone. And so we remain in our seats here in this incongruously plush lobby on the edge of Amazon forest.

"The CIA are an enemy to us," Velasco goes on, "and if it weren't for your friend Alejandro, you would be my enemy tambien." The man's spittle actually flies into my beer. So much for refreshment. Who is right: Velasco, who fabricates a propaganda poster of an American capitalist oppressor, or me, who actually knew the man as my father?

If I were to believe Velasco, my father was like some character out of an Eric Ambler novel, but he wasn't that to me. I think about how Father shouted gringo Spanish and wore brown suits and bought jewels for my mother when he flew in and out of places like Belo Horizonte. To me, he was the kind of husband who endured an anxious and demanding wife; a dad who brought his daughters trinkets from distant places. I see him sipping scotch late into the night at our house in Cali, the theme song from "The Heart Is A Lonely Hunter" winding up the stairwell as Rosie and I, frightened by the ugly end of our parents' marriage, faked sleep in our room. Mother took us back to her hometown on the coast of southern California, and we left Father in South America to sell tires and U.S. Rubber Keds.

Father once said he met Raul Castro at a party but no, I never thought of him as CIA.

"You didn't know my father," I half-heartedly say. I see no point in getting riled. Perhaps by not arguing I can avoid more drastic measures, such as Velasco pulling out his Uzi. How did he put it? *I don't miss when I stick it in the ear.*

Velasco thrusts his face toward mine and his protruding jaw resembles the anaconda over our heads.

"Ask your *novio* Alejandro if you do not believe I know of what I speak."

My *novio*, I see, is in a funk. I turn to Alejandro with the assumption he will leap to my father's defense, but what I get back chills me: The dark impenetrable Ray Bans, the hard face behind them, his total lack of move-ment. He sits as motionless as a cold-blooded iguana, beer in hand, stub-ble darkening his jaw. Clearly he didn't sleep last night, prowling about Mauricio's garden, plotting god-knows-what, assembling his clippings.

"I will tell you something about Velasco," Alejandro says, his words quietly issuing forth, his body rigid as the stone statue of some scary Incan god, "You may say he knows nothing about your father but he knows what it is to be a *desterrado*. He knows of the military tactic known as 'taking the water from the fish.' All of his family was killed in Barranquilla by paramilitary financed by you Americans. It is how it is done. The fami-lies are killed, the land is raped, children are sent into servitude. And in this way the rebels have no resources and the oligarchy wins by killing everything, the country itself, Velasco's people, my Maria." He pauses at the mention of his dead wife but then continues. "And all because you Americans keep doing the drugs, because it is all one big party up there en los Estados Unidos."

I am stunned to silence. Alejandro has informed me of my guilt by nationality and I have no defense. We were to be beyond nationality, I thought, but I'm wrong. I see now how he has been holding back, how his charm and seductiveness has drawn me into this untenable situation in which it is now him and Velasco, clearly a killer, on one side against me, *la gringa*.

"I am very sorry about what happened to your family," I say to Velasco. My words are a feeble apology for so heinous a crime but they must be said, however inadequate. Velasco does not look at me but focuses instead on Alejandro.

"It is a crime, but your corrupt paramilitaries are also to blame," I say, "I'm not your enemy and I'm not my father. Whatever it is you claim he's guilty of, it's not me. I told you I believed in Che and Bolivarian Libertade and if democracy —"

Alejandro slams his palm down on the table. I literally jump, and when I do, Velasco laughs and says something to Alejandro in Spanish I don't understand.

Alejandro lifts up his *Cerveceria Bavaria*, chugs it down, and firmly places the bottle back down onto the table, argument settled.

"I believe in the *comunistas* if it brings good to the people," I whisper, determined to have Alejandro understand that I'm on his side, even if I'm becoming increasingly uncertain as to what his side may be, "And, the FARC, well I don't know how you can defend them after what they did to you."

"You know nothing of FARC," Alejandro says.

"What happened in the forest stays in the forest," Velasco rejoins.

"Whatever you think about my father, you're wrong. He was not the sort of man who would hurt people or let people be hurt. And now," I say and stand, determined to have the final word, "I am going to the room to shower."

"No." Alejandro grabs my wrist, pinches my vein with his thumb.

"Ow!" I try to pull away but he holds on. He looks up at me and smiles in a sweet way I find truly horrifying. He can feel my speeded pulse.

"We are going to *Parque Santader*," he tells me.

"No way," I say, "I don't like you making insinuations about my father." Again I try to pull away, but his thumb digs in so hard I fear I may faint from the pain.

"Ay caribe! La senora esta enfadada!" says Velasco.

"You will love the parrots of *Parque Santader*," Alejandro continues, his voice turning silky, "This is their evening time, this is what you came here to see."

Alejandro rises from his chair, pulls off his sunglasses and looks down into my eyes and suddenly what I see in them is an appeal for me to pay attention. I realize this was all an act, a speech to bring Velasco to his side.

He lets go of my wrist and is turning to speak to the hotel maitre 'd, handing him cash for the drinks and ordering the bags to be taken to our rooms. I look around the café and see another couple, elderly, talking in what appears to be German, and a trio of backpackers grouped around the bar. The bartender smiles as we leave, Velasco standing too close to me, Alejandro taking my hand, and I'm wondering if this is what they will say: "She seemed fine, we thought those men were her friends, it was the last we saw of her."

People are everywhere and I can scream anytime, but I'm not willing to scream just yet, not yet, not until I am certain about Alejandro. He shows himself to me even now between flashes of rage and flickers of brief understanding and despite everything, despite the veiled hints that Father may have been part of something that *must stay in the forest*, I really do want to see the famous parrots of *Parque Santander*.

"You never know how violent a man can be until you put him to the test."

They come in screeching, flocks of bright green wings and feathers fluttering high in the palms and mangroves, roosting in every conceivable tree, hundreds of them. They are called *pericos* — little green parrots — and they dominate the sound waves like a massive 747 soaring in for a landing. Each evening at cocktail hour they come to *Parque Santander* to squawk and scream and nestle into the park trees away from the jungle night predators. I might say I know how they feel.

Alejandro encircles my neck in the crook of his arm and points up into one of the many high palms, as if I need to be shown where all the noise is coming from, and Velasco stands nearby gawking up, hands covering his ears. The *pericos'* cacophony drowns out everything, the voices of other tourists, Alejandro's excited shouting. He is moving me toward a nearby church, ordering Velasco and me to take the stairs to the bell tower where we'll get a better view over their canopy of nesting and screeching. Excited children are pushing us from behind, and suddenly I'm separated from Alejandro, he is behind the children and I'm beside

Velasco who is turning back, seeking Alejandro in the crowd, but we are stuck in this rushing tide racing to the top of the stairs. I see Alejandro stepping back toward a large man in a faded aloha shirt, and then he is gone.

From the bell tower the parrots' shrieks are even louder. A group of children increase the level of cacophony and I can see Velasco tensing, reaching into his pocket. To distract him I point to the birds and he moves toward me. The man is truly frightening. I back away from the railing, afraid suddenly that he might push me. And still the *pericos* fly everywhere, hundreds and hundreds of them, swooping down toward us, delighting the children who join in the screaming, imitating their squawks.

Velasco ducks, his eyes fluttering. He's afraid of the birds, I realize, repulsed by them. I start to walk away but he reaches out and grips my hair at the base of my skull and it's surprisingly effective. I cringe into submissiveness, cry out to be released, though of course I'm not heard. A boy looks up frightened at these two adults, one in the tight grip of the other. Holding me by the back of my hair, Velasco viciously, brutally yanks, pushes and shoves me down the stairs where there are more children coming up, and I submit. We stumble halfway down until suddenly my hair is released and Alejandro is here, slamming Velasco's head against the wall, punching the man's cheek into the stucco.

"Don't you ever touch her like that again, comprendes?"

Alejandro's rage is like nothing I've ever seen. Velasco raises both palms up in a gesture of apology and Alejandro releases him. Velasco nods an acknowledgement of sorts, the acknowledgement that I'm Alejandro's exclusive property. If I ever had any doubt before, I know now how much stronger these men are than me. The power of their attack, the quickness of their fight is, if anything, an education.

"A donde estabas?" Velasco wants to know — *where did you go?* — but Alejandro has the literal upper hand and Velasco is on the defensive as he's told "Yo estuve aqui por atraz" — I was here in back down below. Velasco has no choice but to believe him and I, my veins pumping fight or flight, step down the rest of the flight of stairs.

Alejandro catches up and envelopes me in an unwelcome embrace and I push him away but he won't take no, he's back with his arm around my waist. I try to pull away and move in the direction of an armed soldier patrolling outside the park. More fleets of parrots swoop and scatter and rise in the sky, the din of their calls drowning out my protest — *leave me alone!* — but he won't let go and he shouts in my ear.

"Mira! You do NOT want to do that! Trust me —"

"Trust you! TRUST you?" I shout back, and try as I might, I cannot push his hands away from me, his arm is hard and insistent, the birds drowning out our — by every appearance — lover's quarrel. The soldier glances our way, the assault rifle held casually yet purposefully in his grip. Blandly authoritarian, he looks so young to me, and Alejandro catches my hesitation and steers me clear of him.

"Stay away from me you FUCKER!" I scream at Velasco who follows us still, his face brutal and determined. I massage the back of my aching scalp, my hair I swear is falling out. "Fucking fucker!"

A blond couple with two young toddlers looks shocked by my profanity, but they turn back to their children who are laughing and pointing up at the swirling chattering birds and before I know it Alejandro has picked up our pace, our shadow Velasco close behind.

What did Mother once say? You never know how violent one can be until you put them to the test. It's starting to dawn on me. I should have listened to Mother instead of the wild call of this discordant land, a testament to the whole damn insane return to a place where I mistakenly felt I belonged.

—　—

"For your own protection, don't hurt someone's feelings and not mean it."

Dusk descends with a showy display of maroon clouds as the parrots settle into their palms for the night. I, on the other hand, pace the floor of our Decalodge Ticuna hotel room, jacked up on fury at the man I mistook for a lover. Alejandro and I are at last alone together but whatever desire I might have had for him has been completely obliterated.

"Take this bracelet off me now, I don't want it. In fact, I hate it."

These are the first words I've spoken to Alejandro since we left the screeching parrots of *Parque Santander*. Alejandro produces a tiny key from his pocket and unlocks the bracelet. I slip my hand away, and rub my wrist. He looks into my eyes, but I look away.

"I am very sorry, Mira. You are all right, aren't you?"

This refrain reminds me of someone else I know. They say people pick mates who remind them of their parents, although I would say I have the tendency to go with the opposite. And yet the more Alejandro repeatedly asks me if I'm all right — all right — all right — the more he reminds me of Mother. I wonder how this happened to be, that I ended up with yet another bully. Alejandro is no lover. He's a thug, and I was fooled by memories of our distant past. As with many of the people I have chosen to trust, I find myself once more doing an impersonation of Charlie Brown with the football.

"Mira, please, I —"

"May I have some privacy in the bathroom, please?"

"Certainly," he says, but he follows me to the bathroom door. My scalp still aches from where Velasco pulled my hair, and since the creep isn't here Alejandro will get the force of my frigid, disdainful fury.

"Perhaps you'd like to check the bathroom windows first? Escape routes?"

"No, that is fine." He looks down at the bracelet, turning it over in his hands, like some spurned lover. Gee, sorry I didn't like the emerald handcuffs.

"Oh, good, thank-you," I say and slam the bathroom door so fast it nearly hits him in his apologetic face.

No longer concerned about what is going on, what his problem is, or who the man was in *Parque Santander*, I am simply and plainly focused on one thing, which is bathing, leaving Alejandro at the earliest opportunity, and forgetting his very existence.

As the water runs in the porcelain tub I sit on the edge and sob soundlessly, my body shaking, at all my foolishness. What was I thinking? Rosie was right. No woman of my certain age has any business expecting passion without punishing results, and yet here I am in this border town in the heart of narcoland with some gun for hire drug-runner *or whatever Alejandro is* and his lunatic friend.

But bathe I must, and so I do. I step into the tub and wash away the stink of my fear and my own self-disgust. The bath is hardly what I would call a luxurious or even enjoyable experience although it does serve to rally me. The bathroom is large and clean and the last of the jewel-toned colors of the sky linger at the window.

If I listen I can hear the waters of the Amazon, the street outside grown suddenly quiet by the town's collective preparation before the evening's activities. I wash my hair with the provided spa shampoo, so incongruous, to have shampoo readily available here at the edge of the jungle, a half century's progress from when we traveled as a family, if having a plastic disposable tube for more landfill can be construed as progress.

The bruise-colored clouds fade into night and as I wash and scrub that man right out of my hair and massage away the pain inflicted by his *compadre* I am reminded of my goal to take Father's ashes to the pink dolphins. Father is here with me and I with him, and he is urging me on as he would have done if he was truly alive, and no one, certainly no narco trafficker, is going to stop me. I decide to acquire other travel companions, eject Alejandro from the room. I will find a different tour guide to take me to *Lago Tarapoto*, someone who's never heard of Neruda.

This I plan by the conclusion of my bath and I suppose God is laughing now. I dress in a tank and cargos and twist my wet hair up into a bun and even put on some lipstick. It has grown dark and the air at the open window is still. The parrots are becalmed in the distant trees of *Parque Santander* and I suppose I am too. That is, until I hear the voices on the other side of the door. The men.

I open the door quietly, stealthily, and catch a glimpse of them stuffing the last of several packets of dense, bundled cash into Alejandro's Louis Vuitton shoulder bag. *A single journey can change the course of a life,* I think, recalling the glamorous ad for the expensive luggage. Right. *Or end a life.* I wait for a moment, make a sound so as to alert them, and enter the room.

"Velasco would like to apologize," Alejandro says to me. He puts the Vuitton bag near him on the bed, close.

Head cocked at an odd angle, perhaps because he's choking on his own words, Velasco mumbles a *perdoname Señora* with a sidelong glance. He explains it was the birds that surprised him, the parrots, which was why he pulled my hair; he was saving me from the birds, as in *la pelicula de Hitchcock*, he says. Not for a second do I believe this.

"Okay guys," I say, "What's up? What do you want from Harry Barnes' daughter?"

They resist looking at each other, but Alejandro takes the lead and Velasco lets him do it for a number of reasons, one being his less than ideal facility with English.

"Mauricio —"

"Your boss, yes," I say, eager to cut off Alejandro's *cojones* at any opportunity.

"— decided it would be best that Velasco remain with you —"

"Como tu bodyguard," Velasco says.

"— until a certain event was accomplished to Mauricio's satisfaction —"

"That event being?" I ask. *I don't miss when I stick it in the ear.*

"Es nada importante," Velasco says with an unconvincing shrug.

"You are too modest," I say, and when he looks at me I see pride in his eyes and also how I might manipulate him with that pride, or at least keep him from pulling my hair again.

I wonder, do Colombian narcos behead or not behead, or do they just do *la corbata* or *stick it in the ear* and leave the beheadings to Las Maras of Mexico? This rumination comes to me in a surprisingly dispassionate manner, and it occurs to me that, aside from being in Cali twenty-four hours ago and Michigan forty-eight hours ago, I was also in Los Angeles a little less than a week ago, and that time and place and the person I was seems to have happened in another century.

It's not that I am any less fearful or cautious; I am my mother's daughter still. It's that she's been subsumed by another part of myself; the person Alejandro has encouraged me to be for his own purposes, whatever those purposes may be.

— —

"Sometimes you're lucky but remember,
luck never holds when it's your time to go."

Velasco inspects Alejandro, his supposed *compadre*, for wires before we head out to Discoteca Tacones where Alejandro is to meet with a man named Baranca who may or may not be a *sicario* who may or may not be accepting a cash down payment in a Louis Vuitton bag for his services. This plan of action is what I have gleaned from the bits I picked up in Cali and here in the hotel room as the two men mutter in Spanish and I pretend disinterest. The frisking of Alejandro is quick, just business, and Alejandro doesn't appear in the least surprised by the notion of his brother-in-law Mauricio ordering this thug to follow and keep watch over us, including checking to see if he's wearing a wire.

When Velasco indicates I am next I say *no fucking way*.

"Dude, you are never touching me again," I say, but I'm forced to acknowledge that Senior Mauricio is the man in charge, even if he is far away in Cali. Alejandro offers to frisk me instead. Being a gentleman apparently in this instance, Velasco allows him to do so.

I stand frozen as Alejandro approaches me, his expression apologetic. There is nothing flirtatious or sexy in the way Alejandro runs his hand from just below my crotch down the length of my cargo pants to my feet. He is surprisingly timid, his hesitation having more to do with Velasco's lurking presence than anything I might threaten. There's nothing quite like being shoved and pushed in the middle of two men fighting to realize how much stronger they are.

"I'm here as a *tourista*, not a spy," I say.

Alejandro replies, "It is for your protection."

Protection from you, I think, *and your thug friend.*

With Velasco's instruction Alejandro makes a conscientious tour through the multiple pockets of my J Brand cargos, finding the usual trappings of Kleenex, Tums, and Advil. I may have become an unlikely adventuress, but I remain a hypochondriacal one. This amuses Velasco.

"You don't eat Tums?" I say, opting for conversational banter with my so-called bodyguard, "Don't you ever have too much salsa picante, too much *aguardiente*?"

"Si, pero it is for *maricones*, not men."

"Here, have one, you'll be able to drink more *aquardiente* tonight," I say. I want Velasco to assume I've forgiven him and so I wink at him and peel off a lozenge. This seems to make him my new best friend, and he accepts the Tums for his rumbling *estomago*.

I see in Alejandro's expression as he watches this exchange a glint of either admiration or apprehension or both, but whatever it is, is not for me to care about anymore, as I am done with him. The bracelet — my handcuffs — rests on the dresser glinting green and gold and suddenly Alejandro picks it up and tells me I shouldn't leave it behind. Assuming it belongs to me, Velasco agrees with Alejandro that it would be wrong not to wear it, that someone might steal such an exquisite piece of jewelry if left in the room. I want to throw the bracelet back into Alejandro's face, but I agree to wear it, and when it latches I give him a look that screams my abhorrence.

I slip on a pair of sandals and the chrysoprase necklace I've come to believe I need more than ever. *You gotta be strong, you gotta be together* I sing in my head.

Alejandro produces a can of mosquito repellent and I hold out my bare arms as he sprays me, then himself, then Velasco, like we're ladies of the night dousing ourselves in perfume before slinking out for a high time on the town.

I glance back at my Patagonia roller and remember the most important thing inside it before we leave the room. *I'll be back for you,* is what I think and hold in my mind as we walk down the hall and the stairs and through the lobby with its lit-up green and red anaconda on the ceiling. Soon we're on the street where the stirrings of wildlife in the thick trees beyond the river – <u>the</u> river – hit me like a wake up call that hollers *you're here you're here you're here!*

The party has begun early tonight at Discoteca Tacona. Lights flash across the dark dance floor and the café tables glow with citronella candles. I mark out the other tourists and see the backpackers from the hotel, and one who looks like the young Charlie with tousled hair and lanky frame. I imagine him saving me from my predicament; this boy who could be my son, the incarnation of Charlie taking me away from all this, but as I move in his direction Velasco snatches my wrist. Adrenaline leaps through my body but I fake indifference and to keep him happy I slip my arm through his, this thug killer who nearly pulled half my scalp out.

"Campari and soda, por favor," I say to Velasco as if he's my date, and it works because the man preens with la rubia que todas quieren on his arm, swerves with the heart-and-groin thumping beat of the *vallenato* music. He orders my requested drink and himself a double *aguardiente* and now I understand something else about Velasco, which is that aside from bragging about his marksmanship he also likes to drink. A lot. And *bailar.*

Alejandro orders a beer at the bar and beside him I notice a man I recognize instantly as the one I saw speaking with him at the bottom of the church tower at *Parque Santandar*. The men seem to barely acknowledge one another.

Alejandro follows Velasco and me like a shadow to a table near one of the blasting speakers. The deafening music is fine by me since I'm not here for the conversation but seeking avenues of escape – from Alejandro, Velasco, and the man at the bar who must be Baranca, the *sicario*. I refuse to sit and instead move my hips to the beat, by all appearances eager to dance.

"Quieres bailar?" Velasco asks.

Velasco follows me onto the floor among the lights and other couples where he makes substantial room to embark on his unique imitation of John Travolta. Together we put on a show that is if not spectacular then certainly worthy of amusement if one bothered to notice, although the only person who really notices is Alejandro. When we return to the table Alejandro is looking at me in his most machismo manner: *that look, those eyes*.

Velasco downs his double shot of *aguardiente* and gestures to a waiter for another. But I am back onto the dance floor, surreptitiously seeking the backpackers, the reincarnation of Charlie who has slipped beyond my sights into a crowd of young dancers. Velasco follows me, tiring yet game. The second double *aguardiente* is delivered to our table and when he returns to pay the server I am suddenly whisked into the arms of another dancer. Alejandro.

"Don't touch me," I shout at Alejandro. He backs away, hands raised.

Velasco laughs when he sees our exchange. He drinks his second double *aguardiente* then is pushing back through the dancers to shout out orders to the dj for a repeat of his favorite *vallenato*. The music pounds at us from the speaker near our eardrums and despite my warning Alejandro reaches for my waist and pulls me into him and I don't resist because of the music or maybe the Campari or something as primordial as the river seeping through the jungle outside. For the second time today I'm being yanked and pulled, this time drawn toward the open back door. Alejandro's face looms dark over mine and he kisses me, pulling my body into his.

"No," I say, and pull away, only Alejandro won't let me. He has a hard grip on my waist, his fingers encircling my wrist below the bracelet and I realize suddenly this isn't about desire.

"You must trust me, mia Mira," he says, "Will you trust me?"

"Fuck no!" I say, and turn back toward the *discoteca*, but for the second time today I'm overtaken by someone stronger. He pulls me further outside, yanking me almost off my feet. I try to twist away and scream in frustration.

"Let me go, goddamnit."

"Trust me, Mira," he says again and puts his lips on mine. I bite the flesh on his lower lip and he jerks away but doesn't let go, and suddenly another body is here, the man from the bar, the one I saw with Alejandro in *Parque Santander*.

This is Baranca I realize suddenly and horribly, *the sicario*. This man is bigger than Velasco and Alejandro put together and with him hovering, Alejandro pulls me toward the river, the music thumping behind us, the *Discoteca Tacona* disappearing behind me as if it were a place in a dream.

I start to scream but the man puts his hand over my mouth and my body is being lifted up and I'm being set down into a boat, my screams muffled, my head pushed below a tarp. The smells of boat fuel and burlap rise up into my nostrils and suddenly its Alejandro here again, holding me down, lying on top of me, my face pushed down into sacks and leaves and dampness. He's whispering in my ear, his hand on my mouth, and I'm crying in rage and fury and fear and my words are muffled but their intent is clear.

"Why, Alejandro, why me?"

"You must trust me, Mira."

I laugh through bitter tears, and if I could I would bite his hand, kill him even, but my mouth is gripped tight, my body crushed by his weight.

"What are you? Who are you?" I sob, doubting if he hears me, but he does, and I feel his hesitation, then the words whispered in my ear.

"I am the devil you know."

———

"Everyone needs something to look forward to and someone to love.
But I say people also need something to fear and someone to hate."

———

nighttime cruise on the Amazon was not what I had in mind when I slipped into my Mephisto sandals at the Decalodge Tecuna, but that is what's in store for me now. I feel the boat engine starting up and the rumble on the boards against my chest, and when I struggle to sit up Alejandro cups my nose until I can't breathe, forcing me to lay quiet until his hand loosens and I suck in air through my nostrils. My face may be wet with tears of fear and rage, but I no longer feel either of these things. I am simply numb and vaguely sickened. He pushes his full weight down on me and I can smell his salty sweat and the thick sweetness of beer on his breath.

The boat picks up speed. I'm being swallowed into the jungle like a tiny creature into the maw of a giant anaconda. I think of my mother who will wonder what ever happened to me. I think of my sister and find myself missing her, my sis the doc — what would she say now?

I understand how it is that people make final phone calls to those they love in the end, for this may very well be the end.

"I don't fucking deserve this." My words smash into Alejandro's palm. He hears me and replies.

"No, you do not. I am sorry, Mira. This was not how I wanted it."

He finally lets me go and I rise up but by now we are deep into the river and far from Leticia. The other man is at the helm of the small boat and I can't see his face or Alejandro's face either. The darkness of the river and forest are all encompassing. Somewhere in the far distance I hear the bass beat thundering low and fading from the *discoteca*, but it recedes farther into the river and is drowned by the steady hum of the motor. Tall shadowy trees hang over the water and block out the clouded sky. Creatures large and small call out in the night and the air is filled with miniature flying things and all kinds of unknowable flotsam drifting down from the trees onto my hair and over the boat. I see that my baggage is miraculously here, my suitcase, my purse even, and it gives me momentary hope before it dawns on me: these too will disappear with me.

"So am I going to swim with the dolphins?"

Alejandro's silence is less that of affirmation than confusion. He shifts on the small wood seat, reaches for the baggage and pushes my roller toward me.

"You must put on the boots," he says.

"So I'll sink?"

"Put on the boots."

"Why make it easy for you?"

"Sometimes there are snakes in the boat and the spiders —"

I put on the boots. I'm slipping them on without socks, unable to see well enough to lace them in the dark but assured by their heavy leather toes and thick soles. I recall the instructions that came with them saying they should be worn with a pair of wool socks, cushioned sole, but I'm a beggar not a chooser in this situation. Something delicate lands lightly on my shoulder and I slap at it. It dissolves into a large squishy mass of dead something against my skin.

"We are going to *Puerto Narino*," Alejandro says, "And then we will go on from there."

"Why." My voice is dead; I haven't the will to question. I remember when I once gave my cats flea baths how they would claw and struggle until finally they would give up and succumb, bedraggled and boney in my arms. This is what Alejandro has done to me. If I was given a gun now I wouldn't even be able to kill him.

"Velasco will follow us so we must hide for a while," Alejandro says, "Not long." He reaches into the Louis Vuitton bag slung across his chest. "Turn around."

"No. I'd rather not."

"Very well."

I cringe but then he brings out the dispenser and sprays me with more oily mosquito repellent. Better than a bullet to the head.

"I am not going to hurt you, Mira. I am trying to help you as I help myself."

"Really? Then who is he?" I say, gesturing to the silhouette of the man at the helm, "Is that Baranca? The *sicario* you and Mauricio are paying with what's in that?"

I indicate the Louis Vuitton. Alejandro's face is unreadable in the dark, but I hear him sigh and even laugh a little when he speaks rapidly to the man — "*ella piensa que tu eres Baranca*" — and the man chuckles at my presumably preposterous assumption.

"He is not what you think. He's a friend I can trust," Alejandro says, "An independent working in the spaces between. There are many people in the spaces between."

"Between what?"

"Between cartels, the CIA, the contractors, the paramilitary, the rebels, the counterinsurgents, the drug traffickers. Is this a lovely country or not?"

I hear the ingrained bitterness. Something is happening to Alejandro and I've shown up for the final act.

"I will tell you everything," he says to me, "But not now."

I want to shoot back that I don't care what he tells me, that it's all lies anyway, but instead I carefully lace my boots and let his words sink in. *"I will tell you everything."* It's happening again, that creeping trust — or is it simply familiarity? — with the teenage boy who slipped in through my bedroom window one night after we'd seen Franco Zeffirelli's *Romeo and Juliet* until the neighbors saw us kissing and he was chased away. He had been a romantic boy until being chained to Mauricio changed him forever. Silly me, I think, for wanting that boy and believing in the man he should have grown into.

We do not speak for the next hour or two or more as the boat makes its way further up river. I slap the not-so-little things settling occasionally upon my neck and arms and shoulders then pull out my Ralph Lauren safari jacket and feel oddly absurd slipping it on. It's too hot to begin with, not to mention too fashionable, but then again, so is Alejandro's Louis Vuitton money bag. His handsome silhouette puts him right up there alongside the Bono and Angelina ad campaigns.

I realize I may have drifted off to sleep when the sound of the engine changes and soft yellow lights spark ahead, affording me a clearer view of the glistening tributary and before it the glint of my captor's profile. A windy gust hits the boat as it slows toward a long dock with a few canoes. I can see rows of tidy buildings lining a gently lit street which oddly dead ends at the edge of the jungle. The man at the helm steers the boat into a thicket of trees where a smaller dock, little more than a stub of land and wood, juts out. His movements are automatic, graceful; he throws the line around a stump, pulls the boat in closer. I find my anxiety rising again when Alejandro holds out his hand for mine.

Hobson's Choice. That is what Mother once called it. That's when you have no choice. My no-choice at this moment is to rely on the devil I know. And so I take his hand.

"Some people have the survivor instinct while others..."

Pretty *Puerto Narino*, with its little gardens and sidewalks, however rugged, reminds me of my walk street back in Venice, yet I'm no longer a tourist with the option to stop here. We leave *Puerto Narino* behind in the small rowboat Alejandro has procured from the unidentified man from the "places in between," the man who earns his living escorting drug runners or insurgents or whatever it is that Alejandro is, in this land of the coca.

Our bags have been transferred into the *bote* along with other packages and mysterious supplies, even a microwave ("*por tu seguridad*," the man said), although I doubt we'll be using it to pop popcorn. From my place wedged behind the supplies I watch the man and Alejandro say goodbye, their clasping of hands turning to clasping of arms then shoulders in that unexpectedly emotional way of men who don't expect to be emotional. When they part from their embrace the man hands Alejandro a pistol. Perhaps I'm wrong, but I take it personally, this exchange.

Alejandro pushes off with a long paddle. As the man watches us leave my fear is supplanted by the impression that these men are blood brothers of sorts and have said goodbye forever. It has something to do with

Alejandro having kept the pay-off money intended for Baranca and this
is why Velasco is on our tail. "Hey, it wasn't my idea to take the money," I
want to say but don't say. I'd rather be dancing back at the *Discoteca* with the
red-haired boy, the one that would have been Charlie's son, or my son, if
we had been other people in another place in time.

We float out into the dark of the tributary and I feel the oppression
of the half submerged trees surround us. The swirl of a branch in the
murky dimness above could be an anaconda ready to swing down and
devour me, or it could house one of those Brazilian "wandering" spiders
which crawl into boots and bite you for failing to wear socks, rendering
you dead in an instant.

"I want my phone now," I say to Alejandro.

He ignores me and pushes the paddle through the water. The lights
of *Puerto Narino* fall behind us and now I am truly miserable, and hot, and
sticky, and disgusted. I am disgusted because I have no choice but to feel
empathy for Alejandro, and this is the last thing I want to feel.

"And I want you to take your bracelet."

He faces away from me as he leans into the paddle strokes from his
position at the front of the *bote*, his shoulder muscles moving under his
shirt. The air is bloated with moisture and another gust of wind punches
the water. I think of my family, my friends in Venice, my walk street and
my cats.

"I want my phone," I say again from my perch between the microwave
and my Patagonia roller. I shift my boots uneasily, wonder what creatures may be crawling around in the floor of this boat which had been
sitting there by the man's dock, sitting there for days or weeks while all
things deadly crawled into it.

"First I must make a contact," Alejandro says, "Then I will give it
back to you. It wasn't stolen, it was borrowed, Mira mia."

"I'm not your mia Mira."

"You will always be my Mira. But I will do as you wish. I will take the
bracelet off."

He sets the oar down across his lap and reaches across to take my
wrist in his hands, and quickly, with a flash of a key from his pocket,

the bracelet is released. I pull my hands away so as not to be touched. He shoves the bracelet deep into a front zipper pocket of his jacket and secures it inside.

"What if you can't get a signal?" I say.

"I have back-up," Alejandro says, and taps the pocket with the bracelet.

"You have another cellphone?" I say with a condescending laugh.

"No," he says. "GPS. In the bracelet."

"You put a tracking device in the bracelet?"

"I couldn't risk losing you, Mira."

"So you handcuff me with a tracking device."

"Yes."

"You put a tracking device on me the instant I got off the plane."

"Yes."

He resumes rowing. I sit stunned. Galled. All along, when I thought he'd given me his mother's bracelet out of some deep abiding love for me, his teenage sweetheart, he had been tricking me, keeping me close, like chattel. Free of my golden GPS handcuffs, I dig into my roller and locate the socks, remove a boot, and without touching anything in the boat, slip on the sock and then the boot. Repeat on other foot, rapidly as possible between slapping at the flying things. I pretend I'm in a movie, a romantic comedy, *Romancing the Stone*, which also took place in Colombia, and nothing all that serious is happening in this movie. Alejandro's pistol is a prop, and now this is the part where we banter. But I won't. My throat has willfully tightened. I will not give him the satisfaction of banter.

"The GPS will help them find us," he says, "I am waiting for Dennis to call."

"Dennis."

Here? I want to scream. Dennis who? And suddenly I'm laughing hysterically at the absurdity of it, him waiting for a phone call from some guy named Dennis as he paddles us down into this heart of darkness over a river of poisonous snakes under a sky that is thick and churning with threat of deluge. Anacondas above, piranhas below. And he's waiting for a call from my phone inside the "Hello Kitty" case.

Alejandro laughs too, and because he laughs it's no longer funny to me and so I stop, but he keeps laughing, low and calm.

"Yes, funny after all these years," he says, "Dennis will remember me."

"After how many years?" I want to know but not really, because suddenly this doesn't sound too promising, this awaited phone call from this so-called Dennis.

"Oh," Alejandro says, "Thirty, no, more like forty years."

"You're waiting for a call from someone you haven't heard from in *forty years*? What if he doesn't call? What if he's dead?"

"It is possible but I doubt it. He's in your contacts list."

Dennis on my contact list. In my phone contact list. I start to say I don't know anyone named Dennis, but then *Dennis*, I see him, *that Dennis*, who called me with condolences when Father died. Who delivered the ransom to FARC. The *maybe he's CIA* Dennis.

"Yes, that Dennis," Alejandro says mildly, softly, as though he were dreaming of a children's fantasy character, a big cuddly guy who comes to chase away the bullies who in this case would be Velasco and company.

"You called Dennis? Off my phone?"

"Before we left Cali, I had to be sure."

I am filled with a creeping dread, a certainty that this cannot possibly go well. It is too impossible.

"What did you say?"

"I said I have Harry Barnes' daughter."

Suddenly I leap up, lean over Alejandro and slap the back of his head.

"You've kidnapped me!" I accuse, "I'm a hostage and you've put me in harms way —"

I slap Alejandro again and he turns and grabs at my hands while struggling to hold onto the paddle. The *bote* rocks dangerously. He pushes me back down into the boat and my back hits the edge of the microwave, but Alejandro is holding me up too, pulling me into him, crushing me yet again. *Three's a charm*, I keep thinking, *three is it*. I've been pushed around three times today by men stronger than me and that's it, *three's it*, and I'm not going to take it anymore, but take it I do, for Alejandro has me in his grip.

"You've USED me!" I scream, pushing against him, "You've been using me all along to get to Dennis, to use me, to use me – for Dennis to call."

He releases me so as not to lose the paddle and when he does I slap his face. He slaps me back, quickly and sharp, and I hurl myself at him, my skin stinging. I grab at the paddle, slam it against his chest, try to thrust it into the water, irrationally aiming to throw it away simply because he's wanting to keep it.

"Mira, stop this! Are you not using me too?"

"*Me* using *you*?"

"For your sometime pleasure, –"

"Sometime pleasure! What pleasure? I've been insulted by your pal Mauricio, called a bourgeois American imperialist by him and his idiot narco family, had my hair pulled out by that creep Velasco, been pushed and shoved and now bitten by fucking mosquitoes and dragged out here into the fucking jungle – sure, fantastic, Alejandro, this is lovely, for my pleasure, sure."

I pull again at the paddle, but he holds on.

"You came not for me," he says, using the shaft to separate us and protect himself from me, "Not to see my country, but for me to be your play thing! Is that not right? Am I not a play thing for a bored American princess?"

"Yeah, right." I give the shaft of the paddle a final shove, "I'm so hot for you Alejandro I've decided to become your hostage."

He at least has the modesty to smirk, presumably at his own presumption. In the abstruse light I can't read his expression nor do I want to. I don't want to see the eyes that have manipulated me into this situation.

"*Are* you a hostage Mira? Or have you not come willingly?"

"What, are you kidding me? I was dragged away tonight and kidnapped, fair and square, don't deny it."

"That was for our safety, I had to, I am sorry."

"I was taken against my will."

"Yes."

"Because I'm the daughter of Harry Barnes whose friend Dennis is CIA."

We catch our breath, Alejandro sitting across from me in the boat, me rubbing the center of my bruised back.

"I have wanted to tell you, Mira. All about my life. I have wanted you to know everything. But —"

He stops, stares off. Where to begin, he might as well say, for our lives have been both too short and way too long from when we first knew each other. We have reached an impasse. We are tired of our squabbles, our egos and wants. We are old, used up, and because we are old and used and tired Alejandro dips the paddle back into the water and resumes with our journey, down the tributary, into the forest.

A loud inhuman screech echoes through the dusky light. It's terrifying and beautiful, a pronouncement.

"That is the pterodactyl awakening," Alejandro tells me when I look up with a start. A dinosaur bird? Here? I won't give him the satisfaction of my curiosity, and so I make no response.

The sky is lightening ever so slightly despite the threat of rain. It's been a long night, and now we're approaching dawn.

"I will be leaving this place forever," Alejandro says, "And I have loved it. This is my country. If all goes right with Dennis, I will never see it again."

The dinosaur bird cries out again, a vast thrilling screech of a greeting to the wet shadowy dawn.

"What's going to happen to me?" I whisper.

"You will return to your country and I will — disappear."

There is a rush of wind, a sound of cascading water, and suddenly we are caught in a deluge of rain. Alejandro paddles toward shelter under a thicket of mangroves. The dense leaves shelter us from the onslaught. He moves quickly, flings plastic tarps over the bags and supplies. I realize that he knows this place well, the small tributaries and offshoots from the Amazon, the turns in the river. He unfolds another tarp and approaches me with caution, undoubtedly wary of another attack, but I reach for the plastic and help him unfold it around and over me. He crouches nearby, making himself a small shelter under a poncho. Drops dribble through the tree branches, splattering onto our plastic hoods, and for the time being we have nowhere to look but at each other.

His eyes are watchful; I glance away. The forest disappears behind the downpour of water. It reminds me of San Cipriano when I begged him to take my virginity in the shelter of another mangrove. *How far have we come*, I think bitterly.

"What do you want with Dennis?" I ask.

Alejandro regards me, internally debating, most likely, on whether to share.

"I want him to —" He stops, looks up at the rain, the mist in the air, "To take me in," he says finally.

"In?"

"Into the protection program. You see, Dennis is *my* devil — the devil I know."

"And how do you know Dennis?"

I'm trying to keep it light and conversational as it's the only way I know to get him to spill. By knowing more I may have leverage, even if it's simply the leverage of feeling less used.

"I told you before. It was Dennis," and the look on Alejandro's face is one of — regret? Anger? "Your father sent him with the money to free me from *las Fuerzas*. It was the best and worst that could happen, this big American arriving in the jungle with the money."

Dennis, yes, the big American indeed. He was Father's young assistant at Uniroyal, the family friend all those many years, decades, ago. He was tall and blond, a former Navy SEAL, competitive swimmer and Olympic contender. He picked us up at airports and taught Rosie and me the butterfly stroke at *Club Campestre*. When we flew into Lima for the first time, jet-lagged and culture shocked, he was there to help orient us, and he did the same when we arrived in Cali. Rosie and I both had crushes on Dennis. He was in his twenties then, which would put him in his late sixties now. Dennis came to rescue Alejandro from the FARC, and he will hopefully rescue us now.

"You plan to tell Dennis about —" I stop. There is much I'm not supposed to know; much I don't know.

"Mauricio." Alejandro says. The name drops heavily, like a weight.

"You're going to tell Dennis what that money is for," I say, pointing to the Louis Vuitton.

"How do you know there is money in here?" he asks. I don't know if he's teasing or not.

"I'm observant, what can I say."

"You're the spy's daughter, no?"

"I don't know what you mean." *And I don't want to know*, I realize, not now, not from him.

He smiles at me; fondly, I see, but I don't feel particularly fondly toward him, this man who has put me at risk, who's lied to me by omission, who's clearly used me to get to Dennis. When he gazes into my eyes like this he is trying to make me see him as before but I won't and can't.

"The rain has stopped," I say, and look up, and in that instant a large splat of something — water, I hope, falls onto my cheek.

"But not on you," Alejandro says. When he reaches to smooth the water from my cheek I pull away.

"Don't," I say, "I don't think I like you anymore and so I won't like it."

"Amor es como eso," he says in a voice so low I wonder if I've heard him correctly. *Love is like that.* Like what, I think. Like not wanting to be touched? I pretend I don't hear him and perhaps I haven't.

The bird screeches again. Its call reverberates through the iridescent jungle, an exotic cousin to Grandpa's Rudy Rooster. It is a beautiful wild call. Sunlight reaches the leafy undergrowth and spreads like liquid gold.

I think of how lovely this holiday would have been if not for the inconvenient business of our lives being threatened and him wanting to go into the witness protection program.

"You've used me," I accuse, not willing to let it go, "You've made me feel old."

"Mira, you will never be old."

He says this wearily as he takes up the oar.

"Me," he says, "I am the one who is old. I was born during *la violencia*, and if I do not act there will be more *violencia*. And all because of a beautiful plant with shiny leaves which should have stayed in the forest instead of making its way in all its refinement to your country, which has only made it worse for us. After more than half my life I am done with *la violencia*."

Alejandro pushes the *bote* out from the shore and back into the moving current, guiding it expertly, peering over his shoulder upriver, checking the trees overhead for anacondas and the water for submerged danger and downstream for any sign of human pursuit, and for a fleeting instant I regret the turn of his attention away from me.

But: *love is like that.*

— ～

"Don't eat before swimming.
You could get a cramp and drown."

— ～

W e have set up camp on the farthest shore of beautiful Lake Tarapopo, away from the central access of the tributary. I have been cooperative, silent, quick to take orders. We've assembled the tent Alejandro calls our "*caleta*," built and camouflaged its roof with cut palm leaves, moved the supplies from the boat. Fatigue hits me like a boulder and I realize I had but a short catnap the night before. Now there's not much else to do but wait for Dennis and watch out for Velasco or any others Mauricio will send to come looking for us. Oh, and stay on the alert for any other type of predator, animal or human.

"Be aware," Alejandro says to me, "There are *halcones* everywhere." Falcons, he means, who work for the cartel. I think grimly of Mother saying more or less the same thing. Be aware. Never feel safe.

Please God just get me out of here alive, I think, *and I promise I'll be a better daughter and sister.* How we bargain at moments like this.

Alejandro orders me to take off my boots before I go into the tent. I do what he says, and as I pull off the boots a small piece of cardboard slips out from the heel where I had placed it the day before yesterday — a century ago. The card has instructions for the care of the boots that include directions for how a soldier is to wear socks and keep feet dry to prevent rot and sores. They are instructions for soldiers marching through jungles, Southeast Asian jungles, African jungles, Latin American jungles. They are for rebels and narcos and paramilitary and government soldiers and soldiers on foreign soil. They are instructions for boys, for men, for women and girls too, for children carrying guns or under peril for their lives. I think of when I bought the boots and how I was but some naïve woman with a ridiculous plan of finding passion with an old boyfriend who quotes love poems, and I'm so sickened by the thought of this silly woman that I creep quietly into the tent and curl up and silently sob.

The noonday sun increases the humid heat and beats down upon the tent. Suddenly unbearably hot, I sit up and pull off my t-shirt and pants. I hear Alejandro walking about the tent outside, adjusting the mosquito netting at the entrance. Half naked in skanky underwear and sweaty tank, miserable, inconsolable, I collapse again into my fetal state not caring how my sweaty panic from the night before has dried like a thin scrim of polecat stink on my skin.

"Mira mia, you should drink," Alejandro says. I turn my back to him as he enters and pushes a canteen of water against my back.

"Come, I know you are awake."

"Leave me alone, please," I say.

"No, you must drink water first, then I will leave you alone."

"Fine," I snarl, and sit up and take the canteen and drink. The water is wonderful, never have I tasted water this good and I don't know why this is; I must be feverish or dehydrated.

"Good. Now you must eat this." Alejandro opens a package of waxed paper and suddenly a whiff of something delicious and meaty wafts up and I realize how hungry I am.

"What is it," I say, hesitating to take anything he gives me. It could be drugged, it could be poison, it could be rancid, but nothing rancid could smell this good, this spice-filled.

"It is a beef empanada. My friend packed them for us. We are prepared with enough food for three nights in the jungle if need be, although I don't think it will be for so long."

"You really think Dennis will come."

"Oh, I know he will. But first you must eat. You are starved."

I look at the empanada. It is rolled into a crisp outer layer of crust, and I can see a bit of meat and onions oozing from a break in the skin.

"Why don't you eat it first," I say.

Alejandro looks at me, first disgusted but then bemused, and takes a bite. Hunger pricks at my awareness as he chews but I wait for him to swallow. My mother didn't raise no fool. Finally I take the empanada and devour it, the meat and spice hitting my stomach morsel by morsel; delicious sustenance, life-giving food. He unwraps three more, eating two. I eat the other remaining one, drink more water, and watch him from the corner of my eye, wary that he's seen my tears and will try and touch me again. He doesn't. He just eats. He too is hungry. Is this breakfast or lunch? I wonder. Or maybe this is dinner. Maybe this is all I'm getting. The thought of being so trapped, so dependent on his rationing of the food, makes me furious at him all over again.

"We need to bathe," he says.

"Go fuck yourself," I say, and lie down with my back to him.

"Fine. Stink if you like."

He slips out of the tent. I listen to his footsteps walking away and the sound grows faint, more distant. I wonder how far away he's going, try to remember the distance to the edge of the lake and think it can't be that far.

I close my eyes. The forest sounds rise in a cacophony of insect and bird calls and I despise it all, hate it, wish it would all die so that I can sleep in peace, wish that we big bad Americans could bomb it all back to the Stone Age.

I am awakened by the screech of a bird — the pterodactyl or some other exotic creature. Sitting up, I notice the Louis Vuitton bag and quietly, carefully, open it. What I find inside is not money but instead clippings of orchids, twigs, the cuttings Alejandro assembled in those canvas bags in Mauricio's garden, and I realize this is his luggage, this is what he's taking with him when he disappears. But where is the money? Has he hidden it? From me?

Moving slowly, disgusted with my stink, I slip back into my cargoes and tank and emerge from the tent, careful to close the mosquito netting behind me. I slip into the boots. Heading down the slope, I see the lake is turning golden in the late afternoon light, and I'm drawn to the shore where Alejandro stands looking out. In this instant, shirtless, in a pair of shorts, barefoot, he couldn't look sexier. But then I see the gun tucked into the back of his waistband.

"So what happened to the money?" I ask.

"Money?"

"A Vuitton bag with bundles of one-hundred dollar bills doesn't just mysteriously turn into orchid clippings. Where did it go?"

"Ah, *that money*," Alejandro says, "I gave it to Pacho and it will go to buy books and computers for the children's school in Bonaventura."

"I see."

Sure, I see. This armed and scary guy has donated hit money to finance a children's school.

A breeze stirs off the lake and I'm so disoriented by this new information, I don't know what to believe. What I do know is that I've been beaten down, pushed around, handled, bullied and worst of all, *seduced*, and through it all Alejandro and I have remained strained allies even while the separateness of our adult lives and dissipating countries remain in our blood. How do you escape your own blood?

Blood is what worries me here at the mossy edge of the lake. I remove the boots, dip my toe into the shallow edge of the lukewarm water, and consider the piranhas. Piranhas can tear a person apart and eat her clean down to the bone with her screaming all the way, just like in the movies. And yet my skin is hot and I want to dive in, wash away this residue of fear. The center of the lake reflects the crimson sky. Jade and bluish colors of the jungle rim its cool borders. The water beckons me to swim. If I survive I'll crawl back into the tent for another good sob, although I no longer feel like sobbing.

And then I see it. A slither of movement, a long sleek fish of a body skims just below the surface of the water then disappears. I don't know if I've merely wished it to happen or if it's real. Then I see it again: A pink creature with a grin breaks the surface and dives.

"It's a dolphin!" I whisper.

I turn to Alejandro standing a short distance from me. When I turn back to the lake it's gone, a gentle ripple in its wake.

"The dolphin, he wants to swim with you," he says.

"What makes you think it's a he?" I challenge. We wait and watch, but the surface remains still.

"I don't," he says, and looks at me sidelong. "Perhaps he is like me."

The lake dazzles, a giant Amazonian jewel, and somewhere beneath its shimmer are creatures like none I've ever seen. They sing, *We are alive, you and I. Alive! Este momento, ahora, aqui!*

"Dive in," he says, "Swim out to him."

"Now I know you're trying to kill me."

"I thought you wanted to see the pink dolphins."

"What about the piranhas?"

"They are also called *caribe*, and they are good for eating. They are here but they won't harm you if you aren't bleeding."

"Why should I trust your word," I say.

"Don't then. You may wash with this if you like."

From the pocket of his trunks he produces a kerchief and holds it out to me with a look of tolerant patience. I don't take it. Instead I listen to the discordant bird calls pronouncing the day's end and think of how soon I will have to climb into the tent and spend the night with this man. I want escape, if only for a moment; I want to swim into the lake and dive down among the pink dolphins.

I fling off my top, strip off my cargos and underwear; stand naked in the twilight.

Before I can talk myself out of it, I dive in.

Ripples massage and cool my skin. Heart thumping, I swim the short way out to where I saw the dolphin and wonder if this is my final moment on earth and how sublime it would be until the *caribes'* little mouths would come digging into my flesh. I keep swimming, thrusting my arms into the water. Just at the moment I can't stand the terrifying certainty that I've gone too far, that *this is the end*, I feel a body brush by.

"There he is!" Alejandro shouts from the shore, "Behind you!"

Treading water, I turn. The dolphin breaks the surface with his smiling long-nosed face. Truly fleshy pink, opalescent, it — he — looks at me with small dark eyes then dives. I feel the power of his body rushing past me in the water.

"Play with him! He wants to play!"

The pounding inside my ears muffles Alejandro's distant voice. The dolphin circles me, brings his snout within inches of my face, again looks right at me. He flips his tail and dives in a whoosh of wavelets skimming my flesh.

Come play, he indeed is saying and I will, I do.

I dive to seek him underwater, open my eyes. Through wavering viscous emerald light I see the dolphin again, a streak of pink coming toward me, nodding his head, whipping his tail, whishing past me fast, the current stirring bubbles. I surface to grab a breath and dive again, but the dolphin is gone. Then he is back, coming at me from behind; he appears delighted with this trick. I am in the dolphin's medium and game to play yet when I dive again he disappears — *ha ha!* I surface for another intake of air and what I mistake for another dolphin turns out to be Alejandro, naked, diving, his feet kicking the surface. He disappears underwater, dares me to follow, and I do. He is my childhood companion, the boy I could out swim. Underwater, I signal to him — *there!* I've spotted the flipping tail, and in a burst of our human feet and arms, kicking, paddling, we swim toward the dolphin and see it thrusting up, a rosy flash in water turning burgundy in twilight. We grasp more air, laughing, shouting. The dolphin tosses his head as if laughing too and again dives, taunting us to play at being dolphins, a game we played in the rapids of San Cipriano, and we follow, diving and surfacing, then diving again.

Time melds the now with decades long gone and in this moment it seems we could start over with who we were before we were changed, yet that would be impossible for time keeps moving, and before we know it the lake is wine dark and the dolphin has disappeared into the vermillion depths to swim home to wherever home is in the abyss of *Lago Tarapoto*.

I've had about all the thrills I can stand. The lake turns from scarlet to a deep murky green. From underwater I see a flash of Alejandro's legs and before surfacing I pinch his knee, another game from our youth. He shouts, surprised, this man with the same arched feet he had as a boy. He swims beside me on our way back toward shore, our bodies naked and close, pulling the water, our strokes pumping in tandem.

We step out onto the sand and the thick warm air caresses our skin. I turn and look at him, his feet and his legs and thighs. I look at how erect he is, water rushing off his abdomen, dripping down through his black hair. He faces me and waits. I push a wet tendril back from his brow. His face, his skin, gives off heat. Still he waits. Have the birdcalls in the forest gone instantly silent or has all sound been eclipsed by the singular surge of his breath?

I take his hand and hold it for a second. *Friends*, the gesture says as I move closer, face to face, body to body. Then I move his hand to the center of what has dared me to be fearless, and he strokes me gently, our mouths coming together in a deep wet kiss. I will possess him now, my hand along his back, across the crevice of his buttocks, along his thighs. I grasp him and we are laughing a little because we are falling into each other, stretching out onto the mossy sand. The *caribe* could devour my trembling toes dipped in the water's edge but it would all be worth it to have this, *now*, the call of birds and jungle, my fevered body rising in pitch. I roll him under me. He gives himself over to me, my back arching under the black-forested sky, and we push toward an ending I want to forestall yet can't — my life, his life, our blood and yearning, racing to a conclusion we cannot avert.

— ⁓

"You can only be betrayed by people you trust."

— ⁓

Stars break out in a pitch-black sky. We lay side by side on the cool moss and he takes my arm, pulls me close, both of us naked. We have bathed again in the lake afterwards, drying our skins in the warmth of the evening air. We hear far away calls that I can only imagine belong to large man-eating creatures. Closer still, I hear chattering, clicking grunt-like sounds.

"What's that?"

"Ah, those are the *guaguas*."

"Okay, so what are *guaguas*?"

"They are giant rats."

Alejandro laughs softly at my sudden urge to hurry back into the *caleta*.

"Acuérdate de este momento," Alejandro says, his mouth brushing against my ear. Stop for this moment. Remember this time. "There will never be another like this one."

This is true. I will never again make love on the shores of *Lago Tarapoto* with piranhas lapping at my feet. Nor swim with a pink dolphin or see the Southern Cross winking through the tree canopy or smell the sweet verdant exotica of the Colombian jungle. When but hours ago I wanted nothing more than to escape Alejandro, now I will never get enough of him. *Este momento.*

I turn onto my back and let the stars draw me up into the universe. Alejandro's arm rests across my chest, pinning me here to the ground where insects move beneath in the vegetation, undoubtedly preparing to chow down on my backside. But for now, just now, I will pretend we're at a picnic without ants — or spiders — or man-eating fish and bigger creatures coming down to the lake from the forest. *Este momento.* If I live through this what I'll want to remember is the stars and Alejandro's skin and his face close to mine in the dark and the whisper of his breath at my ear when he says *este momento*, not my heebie-jeebies over a few bugs, or many bugs.

I roll over onto my stomach and kiss him on the mouth.

Inside the tent Alejandro lights a citronella candle on the floor between us and wraps me in mosquito netting, stroking my neck with a small possessive smile, shushing me to be still when he pulls a spider from my hair. Lovely, our little hovel.

He tosses me a small wax bag of Brazil nuts, and while I ordinarily pick the Brazil nuts out of a mixed bag, I chew them ravenously.

"Save *algunas para mi*," Alejandro says, busy with sifting through a sack of supplies, pulling out a canteen of water.

It crosses my mind that we will have to survive together for however long it takes, a day, a week, months. Some people spend years in the jungle waiting for rescue or freedom. This is one of those cases of making your bed and lying in it. I've been abducted by desire and so I must be on board for the duration.

"Here then," I say. When I pass the nuts back to him he shifts the dark object in his left hand to the other and I see that it's the gun.

"Will Velasco come looking for us tonight?" I ask. I try to keep my voice neutral, I try to comprehend that the gun is meant to protect *us*, not hurt me. This man just made love to me; he would not hurt me, why do I think he will hurt me? Because he can and he will if he must. But he won't 'must.' There is nothing that I will do that will make him want to hurt me.

"No," he says, "But we will be cautious."

The candle flickers on the floor of the *caleta*, and because I can see only the shadows in Alejandro's face I rely on his voice to fully understand the level of threat.

"What kind of gun is that?"

"Walther PPK," he says. He tilts the Walther so I can better see it by candlelight.

"Oh, sure, PPK," I say, "Makes all the difference. PPK."

Alejandro looks up to see if I'm kidding and smiles just a little when he sees I am.

"It is from my friend Pacho."

"Do you think Mauricio will send others to find us?"

"They won't find us. This is my special place."

"That's why you have the gun."

"Yes."

His short declarative answers are beginning to get to me.

"What really happened to the money?" I say.

"What money?"

"Did you really give it to your children's school in Buenaventura?"

"Ah, that money."

"I know there was hit money in that bag," I say, "Instead of orchid clippings."

He sets the loaded gun on the ground behind him and reaches for the bag of nuts, the candlelight illuminating his face. He says nothing, his expression neutral, devoid of expression even. His resolution is one of resistance to me. He will not be forthcoming, and so I push.

"Maybe you need to tell me more," I say.

"I think it is better that you don't know much."

"Aren't you curious to know what I do know?"

He leans his back against a rucksack, stretches out his legs in front of him, and chews a nut slowly and casually.

"If you would like to tell me, Mira, yes, I will listen."

I take a breath and hesitate before I start. I could begin with what I overheard at Mauricio's house in Cali, continue on to what I understood happened at the hotel in Letitia when he and Velasco stuffed the cash into the Louis Vuitton, and end with what I've concluded, which is that Alejandro was supposed to pass the money on to some *sicario* named Baranca. Alejandro chews and with that neutral expression waits for me to speak. He is smart, calculating, no longer my warm cuddly lover. The love-making was good, I think, but sex won't make him talk.

"You owe me an explanation," is all I say.

"Perhaps."

"I think —" and now I stop. How do you say "I think you are planning an assassination" to a man with a loaded Walther who has just told you it's better to know nothing, or pretend to know nothing?

"I know more than you think," is all I manage.

"Very good, Mira."

He has just praised me for keeping my mouth shut. Aren't we supposed to trust one another? Did what just happen by the lake not change everything?

"You do know, don't you," I say, "That American girls don't just put up and shut up."

"And Latino men are not *gringa* playthings. We played at dolphins like children but that was only for a while, Mira. We are not playing at espionage like they do in your movies."

"Who said anything about movies?"

"Lie down, Mira."

"No, I want you to tell me more."

"I will tell you later. Lie down."

"*Make me*," I whisper. He comes up to me and takes both my wrists in his hands as I am thinking, *good, the gun is over there.* He pushes me back down upon the ground and puts his full weight on top of me and kisses me. His face is warm, hard and bristled. I open my mouth and receive and caress his tongue with mine. I want more but he stops.

"When you don't tell me anything, when I can't participate," I say, "You make me a hostage, don't you see?"

His eyes darken.

"That is up to you. When Dennis comes you can tell him you are here against your will or you can tell him you came willingly. That is your decision, Mira."

He rolls off of me, turns his back to me and blows out the candle. We are plunged into darkness. I know he is shifting to locate the gun securely within his reach, and I hear the rustle of mosquito netting as he pulls it around him, shifting and reclining onto the ground with his back to me. No more kisses.

I'm being punished for wanting to be an equal partner. *To hell with him,* I think of the man I want more than safety, comfort or security. I want him so badly I have no choice than to roll over onto my stomach and pray for sleep as the jungle sounds rise up in symphony and slowly, slowly, the man's breathing deepens and he sleeps.

You can always count on a man to fall asleep in the middle of an argument.

— ∙ ∼

"Don't take candy bars into the tent because a bear can attack you before you even get out of your sleeping bag."

— ∙ ∼

Something has awakened me.

I hear it again. Footsteps walking through the leaves, crunching softly, stealthily, moving close to the *caleta*. Terror grips tight at my throat and I can barely breathe. I reach across to warn Alejandro, touch the spongy netting encircling his arm. He awakens quietly; I hear his breath stopping to listen. And there it is again, the sound of footfalls on leaves. *Crunch, crunch crunch.* Alejandro reaches for the gun. I close my eyes. I don't want the mosquito netting with its bits of twigs and insects crawling its surface to be the last pathetic thing I see in this life.

The footsteps move away but not far, then return. It's more than one person, two maybe, although they don't speak. Now they are circling the tent. Something large pushes up against the leafy camouflage, and then I hear a snort, a sniffing, and realize that it's an animal, not human. At first I'm relieved but then a rush of alarm like nothing I've ever experienced courses though me. *An animal.* Not human. Humans can at least be reasoned with, up to a point.

An animal. A large hungry one with teeth that can rip into the tent and then my flesh, an animal which can render my demise so horrifying and terrible as to make death by piranha seem like a walk in the park. I want Alejandro to shoot it, shoot it right now; I don't care what it is, just kill it. I can practically see his grip on the Walther, feel his finger itching to do it, but instead he waits and listens. The animal walks, yes four-legged it is, back and forth at the entrance to our *caleta*. It sniffs and nudges the palm leaves, not fooled, knowing something is inside here. Us.

I bury my face into the pallet that is my makeshift bedroll and stifle the urge to cry out. Alejandro shifts quietly to my side and then he's on top of me, spreading his entire body over my back, a human shield. *It will kill him first* I think wildly, an absurd consolation, *it will have to kill him to get to me.* But he will shoot it before it gets me, and he will die first if need be and I am a coward, a grateful coward, lying beneath strong hard Alejandro, and I want to scream *don't let it kill you, just shoot it,* but instead he waits.

Amazingly, after one final snort, the animal's soft, elegant footsteps retreat. I hear running paws thumping and the swooshing of shrubbery in its departing wake.

"Jaguar," Alejandro whispers into my ear.

Now I'm glad he waited for it to leave and didn't shoot it.

So the big cat was merely inspecting the new residents, concluding perhaps that there are better ways to catch dinner than attacking armed humans.

Alejandro remains on top of me. I feel his grip loosen on the Walter and he releases it, his right hand moving to touch my shoulder. I breathe shakily, face down into the bedding, and reach up to clutch his hand, a signal that says *don't move* and he doesn't. His body is a heavy blanket of human contact, pushing me down into the pallet, and soon my backside is moving, undulating into him. *Ah Mira* I hear, his hand moving down to pull away the tangle of netting that separates us.

⁓ ⁓

"People with secrets are dangerous."

- -

F ather once said *people are dying to tell you their stories.* He was referring to the technique of getting people to talk; eschewing the notion of waterboarding or torture. It was a hypothetical conversation. Or so I thought.

In the case of Alejandro, it was the jaguar that did it. The black cat guided us to a viewpoint along the River Styx that happened to be the *Amazonia*. Primal fear tore down the final barrier. Alejandro would have died to save me, and I would have fought to save him. Leave it to the prospect of being ripped apart by kitty claws to get him talking.

"You are my compañera," he says to me.

We are entwined in each other's arms in the pitch darkness of the tent, unable to see each other's faces and with only the touch of our bodies and sound of our voices to weigh if we are speaking the truth-the-whole-truth-and-nothing-but-the-truth. I roll onto him and say, *yes, I am your compañera.*

"Tell me," I say, "About the years I have missed." My lips are on his throat and I can feel his heart beating there, "You know I must know."

"No one knows." His whispered reply is a vibration against my mouth.

"Someone's got to know," I say, "and it might as well be me."

I feel the tension in his fingers against my shoulder and keep my body draped over his, not moving. He begins with a long sigh of release.

"I say I am a landscape designer but this is only a part of who I am. I have been other things. A traitor to both sides and to myself."

He stops. I don't move or speak or even allow him to hear me breathing. I am an ear that receives his voice, a mind that listens and waits.

"Much will come out in these government peace talks, and many who worked inside against *las Fuerzas,* people like me, will be outed," he says, "And so you see, what stayed in the forest for so long will come out of the forest and I will be a dead man."

"Dennis will come for us."

"Ah, good ol' Dennis."

He's starting to clam up again, I think.

"So you worked against the FARC?"

"Is that what I was saying?"

His voice goes cool but still he hugs me close in the dark. I feel his body struggling to release a hard secret woven tightly within. I wait until he speaks again.

"Mauricio and I became close like brothers when I was captive. He was with *las Fuerzas* but he was young like me, so the leaders chained us together to a tree. He was one of those rich kid *revolucionarios,* and they made fun of him. I knew him from the soccer competitions. We both were the landowner class."

"Our school played soccer with Medellin."

"Yes, and Mauricio, he was a sports star for a time, until he got all *revolucionario* crazy."

"So you recognized him, when they kidnapped you."

"Oh yes. He confessed that it was he who said they should kidnap me, because he knew my father was with Uniroyal. They liked that, it meant taking ransom from *los Estados Unidos.*"

"You befriended him?"

"When you are chained like that for days and days, everything changes. He thought he turned me into a *revolucionario* like him, and after a week it was hard to say who was prisoner and who was not. The rebels were hard on Mauricio but he was loyal to them. They have repaid him over many years with protection for his coca."

"But you worked against FARC?"

His fingers clutch my hair, my head is pinned against his chest and my thumb upon his clavicle feels the thumping of his blood. I want to see his face, but night presses upon us. I have no sense of when dawn will come; it seems the darkness of this night will last forever.

"*Las Fuerzas* killed my father slowly," he says, "He never recovered, he died slowly for years, and so I wanted revenge. Because I had befriended my captors, Mauricio especially, it was possible to get inside. I wanted to punish them all, so I passed on the location of rebel hideouts, anything Mauricio told me. He was out of *las Fuerzas* by then, paying them with coca, but still he told me everything. He trusted me."

"Because you married his sister," I prompt.

"Mauricio was my brother, but I was conspiring against him, never telling Maria. But when she was killed my former employer became my enemy."

I sense something momentous dawning, something I don't want to know but must know. I'm overheated; my mouth turns dry.

"Who was your former employer?" I ask, dreading my own question even as it leaves my mouth.

"You know who it was."

"No," I say, "No, I don't."

"You must know your father was CIA."

"No, I don't think so. That's impossible, he wasn't that kind of guy."

"And what kind of guy is that?"

Father. My dad. The Uniroyal tire and Keds salesman. I try to jerk away but Alejandro holds me in a close clinch, and now I'm getting it, everything I wanted to know. There were things about Father I never understood and I'm to understand it all whether I want to or not.

"It was your father who recruited me to work against *las Fuerzas*. He and Dennis, after I came back from *Universidad*. Yes, Mira. Your father was CIA."

"I can't believe it. My father wasn't —"

"A foreign agent?"

"Father would never have approved death squads," I say. *Not Father. Not my father.*

"No. By the time the death squads happened, he was retired back in the U.S."

Suddenly I wish with every fiber of my being that I could tell my father what I know, tell him I've discovered his secret life manipulating the politics of other countries. It makes sense, we always suspected, when I think of the hotspots we had lived: Guatemala in the late fifties; Iran in the time of the Shah; Peru before the military communist junta; Colombia during the growing emergence of FARC.

"Your father convinced me to bring to the CIA many of *Fuerzas'* secrets," Alejandro says, "and they repaid me by killing my wife."

The whispered words tumble into my ear and if I were to try and wrench myself out of his grasp he could break my neck in the crook of his arm.

"The CIA didn't kill Maria," I say, but then I have to add: *"Did they?"*

"The war against the *Fuerzas,* your father's war, it slipped out of our hands. U.S. money went to the paramilitaries that killed her. Paramilitary men like Tinto Pasquez wanted the coca just like the *Fuerzas* wanted it, and both were killing the farmers, the small ones and big, and landowners, people like my Maria."

"But you said Father never — he — it must have killed him, to hear it was all going to hell."

"Your father was a good man, but good men can start something that later becomes complicated."

"Good men like you?"

"I am not a good man. Maybe once I was good, but not after, not after Maria was killed, shot in the head like an animal by a piece of filth that wanted her land and decided to play God. It was not her time. She was beautiful and alive, and this Tinto Pasquez took her life when it was not her time and so he had to pay."

A part of me wants to stop him from telling me, but it is inevitable if I must know all there is to know about Alejandro.

"He paid — how?"

"I joined with Mauricio," he says, "And we had a *sicario* take him out."

Take him out. He has confessed to murder. Alejandro has participated, with Mauricio, in the murder of a man. A justifiable homicide, a homicide outside the law; the killing of a man who killed his wife.

"Okay," I say, attempting to keep my voice calm and level. *Okay I hear you.* "I'd do the same if I were in your position." *Or would I?*

"I am not a good man," Alejandro says again, wistfully, almost philosophically, his words coming at me, his mother confessor. "Revenge is what my life became about. First for Papa, than Maria. But the trouble with revenge killing is if you are a man like Mauricio it does not end. *I am only the gardener,* I said to him, *I will plant your garden but do not tell me about the killings.* But of course that is impossible. Now I know what I know and I must stop it."

"What? What must you stop?"

He turns sideways on our *palleta* to face me. It's getting light, and I can see the older lined and drawn face of the man he is. This is not who he set out to be and yet the other part of him that is beautiful is still there, at least to me.

"Mauricio is preparing to kill a judge who speaks of extraditing traffickers. If this happens, if the judge is killed, the peace talks with the *Fuerzas* will not happen. You see, after so many years of secrets in the forest, many will be talking, and so I too I must talk."

"Have you warned him? The judge?"

"No. The phones are tapped, my every move is watched, and there is corruption everywhere, in my own government."

"So you need Dennis to help stop this killing."

"I remember Sicilia, this judge, I met him at a party once," Alejandro says, "He is a good man with a kind wife who has a library for barrio children in Cartegena. People like the Sicilias are good for my country and Mauricio, who is my brother, who I once loved, he is just bad. I will tell Dennis and the hit will be stopped and so will Mauricio and his *sicarios*, Velasco, all of them. If Dennis comes."

I stroke his face; feel the coarse bristles.

"Dennis will get us out," I say.

"This is where you come in, Mira," he says, "This is the part you will not like."

"Okay. So tell me."

It is light enough for me to see his eyes. He grasps my fingers. I'm listening, he's talking. It's what I wanted.

"Last month when I was wondering how I could stop this killing I saw your name in a magazine."

So it wasn't serendipity, our meeting. Of course not.

"Garden Design."

"There could be only one Miranda Barnes who — how did they say it — whose 'plant palate is inspired by the tropical South American countries where she lived.'"

"Those articles make people seem so different. When I read it I didn't recognize myself."

"Well, I recognized you, I knew it had to be you, the girl I knew, the girl whose father was CIA."

"And so to find Dennis you arranged to have our meeting look like a coincidence," I say, trying hard to avoid the accusatory tone.

"Isabella wanted her wedding to be in Newport Beach, so I called your associate Magill."

Alejandro says this in the most modulated tone, silken and mild, as if he were discussing the color of wallpaper, "And when I stayed at your home that night, I was hoping to find Dennis on your phone's contact list. I needed an inside way."

"I was your inside way."

"But then your mother surprised us that morning —"

"Good ol' Mom!"

"Later I sent Dennis a message when I borrowed your phone during the garden tour, but he never called. Then you agreed to come."

So Mother correctly suspected Alejandro. Did Margaret wonder if her husband was really selling tires and Keds? Perhaps she couldn't comprehend the source of her anxiety, and so amid military coups and rebel kidnappings she fretted over her children choking on fish bones.

I embrace myself, wrap my arms around my chest, keep myself close.

"You lured me to Cali so you could contact Dennis," I say, "Force his hand."

Alejandro rolls onto his back and knows better than to try and touch me now.

"Yes, but when Mauricio discovered you were Harry Barnes' daughter I had to convince him I was holding you hostage to keep the CIA off our backs before he took out Sicilia."

"So complicated, how could you stand it? The lying to me, the lying to Mauricio."

"Mauricio decided to test me," Alejandro continues, "By ordering me to make the cash delivery to the *sicario* Baranca for the hit. And he decided Velasco would place you in danger to keep me on his side. But he pushed me too far. No one, no one will hurt you. I will not allow that to happen. If you were hurt, that would be the end of me."

I stare up at the ceiling of our *caleta* and can see the outline of mangroves against the morning sky and the shadowy shapes of insects crawling across the sheet of mosquito netting. The air is moist and full of teaming life and here we are, side by side, together in the Amazon. I try to digest it all, everything: Alejandro's desperation, how ridiculously infatuated I must have seemed back in Venice, how Alejandro used that infatuation.

"I am sorry, Mira," Alejandro whispers, "I will never hurt you."

I reach across what seems like decades and nations at war to take his hand.

"So what are you going to do to me now?"

"What would you like me to do to you?"

I roll onto my side and put my hand on the warm blood pumping part of his neck above his clavicle, the part of this man's body I have always found beautiful.

"You used me," I say. His chest rises and falls under my arm.

"Yes, *mi* Mira. I used you. But I've wanted you too, want you, you must know that."

Does he really? I wonder, and why should that matter? Do I want my captor to desire me before I'm sacrificed to the rainforest?

I push away the last shred of mosquito netting protecting my body. My skin flushes and my breasts are damp and my stomach, pelvis, even my feet, are hot.

"You used me," I say to the man on the *palleta* beside me, but it is not an accusation. "So use me again, Alejandro, use me up."

He leans over me and looks down into my face and then begins what started it all when we were young, when even the cool shadow of the waterfall couldn't extinguish our heat.

— —

— ~

*"You should always carry epinephrine on trips
in case you have an allergic reaction to a sting."*

— ~

Morning has come to the forest.

We eat nuts and fruit and drink water instead of coffee, and
while I miss my creature comforts I know *este momento* is all
we have together. Down at the lake pink dolphins leap into the sunlight,
their mouths laughing in the brilliance of this day.

Alejandro is astonished when I bring out the CVS bag of Father's ashes, then he helps me release them into *Lago Taropoto*. Handful by handful,
the ashen remains of all that's left of Harry Barnes passes through our
fingers, falls onto the surface of the water and sinks. I think of the year
we left Father behind in Cali and how the years moved us along in our
separate countries and places and it seems more than strange to think
that all this time, while I thought he was selling tires and Keds, Father
was conspiring against communists and drug lords in South America.

How true it is that the dead take with them their secrets.

Alejandro pours the last of my father's ashes from his hand and I tip
what's remaining from the CVS bag into the lake.

We never truly know the people we love. I wonder about how Father came to his secret life as he traveled through Latin America and the Middle East, how as an American he brought his pocketful of dreams from a farm in Ohio to end here in the heart of the Amazon. I remember his low laughter and booming voice, see him walking the wheat fields of his boyhood farm and the hard concrete of Sixth Avenue in Manhattan. He drove a VW Beetle on the slippery slopes of the Andes. He gently laughed when his culture shocked daughters cried into their piss yellow Inca Colas. I see him appraising Mother's fashionably black "witch boots" in Paris and I see him beaming with joy on the day he married Gloria who gave him a second chance at love justly seized. And while he is not in the photographs he took of us in Istanbul, Milan, Rio, Tegucigalpa, Lima, his presence is there in their composition.

I wonder who he was and will know only some of who he was.

He let us all go by being the first of us to leave, and because he is in the dolphins and the river now he isn't really gone. He just isn't coming back.

＊　－

"Don't get hit by a stray bullet meant for someone else."

＊　－

Colombian men with assault rifles break through a bamboo thicket and there's a tall American among them, older, with a grey buzz-cut and the broad shoulders of a lifetime swimmer. Dennis. The young military men in fatigues raise their weapons and point them at Alejandro, but I hear Dennis' words of warning — *cuidado, el es amigo de ella* — and then his request that I assert this.

Alejandro has raised his hands. My hands too are raised. It's what one does when a soldier points a gun at you.

"Esta bien," I call out, "El es mi amigo."

The soldiers lower their weapons. Dennis walks briskly toward me and pulls me into a hug, and suddenly I'm crying, it is too much, Father's old friend here at last, it's too much.

"It's okay, Miranda, you're okay," Dennis says.

As it turns out, Dennis remembers everything. He remembers Alejandro was my old boyfriend. He remembers the boy's anger at FARC for shooting his father, and he recalls using that anger to later recruit him. He remembers Father befriending Alejandro long after his wife and daughters returned to the U.S., and how he cultivated the friendship until as a young university graduate Alejandro agreed to work undercover for them. He remembers how baffled and tormented Harry Barnes had been when paramilitaries killed Maria, and how they ended up losing their FARC undercover to the other side.

On the five kilometers hike to the airstrip in the middle of nowhere Dennis chats about my father as through he were walking beside us. Harry had seen the Taj Mahal and the Caspian Sea and the ruins of Machu Pichu, Dennis says, but *Lago Tarapoto* and its dolphins remained the last on his list of places he had always wanted to see.

"I should have known," I say to Dennis, "All that time when you were teaching us to swim the back stroke at *Club Campestre,* that a former Navy SEAL wouldn't really be selling sneakers in Cali."

Dennis has a hard-ass smile and commanding presence that none of us, not Alejandro or the Colombian military soldiers, would want to take lightly. I suspect Dennis became part of a new war in South America that Harry Barnes saw spiraling beyond his control. Father had played his hand. He took the pictures, got the passports, crossed the borders. He urged us to travel and explore as if knowing his daughter would somehow end up here with Alejandro and that Dennis would arrive to bring us "back in company."

The world is big, Harry Barnes would say to me now, and life is too big to waste on not feeling safe.

— —

— ⁓

"When you say good-bye to your friends know
that you may never see them again."

— ⁓

They call this is an airstrip, this postage stamp sized patch of land
cleared in the jungle, but what I imagine is the Cessna failing
to rise high enough over the surrounding trees and crashing
with Alejandro onboard. We hold one another in a final embrace but it
won't change the outcome, which is that soon we must let go and he will
board the Cessna with Dennis and I will be escorted into a helicopter by
a Colombian military soldier.

"I don't like saying goodbye," I say.

"Perhaps you should try it, Mira."

"No, I can't, I won't. I'll see you again, I know it."

"Siempre estaremos, tu y yo, solos sobre la tierra."

Neruda: We shall always be, you and I, alone upon the earth...

It took our lifetimes to find our way from goodbye as children to this
second goodbye as adults at an airstrip clearing in the Amazon. The first
time he left his nation in the throes of civil war and now this time he is

leaving to ensure its peace, and still again Colombia is separating us. *Siempre estaremos.* We shall always be.

I say I want to be with him even though I can't possibly. However much I've assimilated the notion of living instead of dying in these scant seventy-four hours it has led me back to my own life, not his.

His eyes sweep over the details of my grimy face, stringy hair. He looks to my lips and kisses me softly then not so softly. He steps back from me and smiles. His dark face glows. I try to do it all; see him and be *en este momento* as it moves forward without turning his face and voice into a memory, but life is not about stopping time, it's about living it now and letting it pass. Time is Dennis waiting in the periphery and the sound of the Huey rotor whipping the air and the soldier whistling a call to the pilot. I feel the weight of something Alejandro has slipped into my pocket and then he is saying one more thing, one last precious string of words.

"Pay attention, Mira. Abre tus ojos and you will know how to find me."

Abre tus ojos. Open your eyes.

The rotor roars over my head and I can't believe I'm allowing my feet to walk me away from him and that he is walking away from me toward Dennis. We move to our separate conveyances, the wind from the shrill rotor nearly blowing me off balance. I will Alejandro to turn around and he does, and for just one more time I see his face. Dennis waves, ready to get on with it, company man Dennis with his cool blue eyes. Alejandro shouts something that sounds like *hasta luego*, but I can't hear it. I nearly run back to him but instead I'm shouting *adios hasta mas tarde.*

Goodbye until later.

The Huey lifts up and through the opening I see Alejandro standing beside the Cessna looking up, his hair whipping in the draft. His face gets smaller until he's a figure below in the clearing in the dark green jungle and then that figure disappears into the Cessna to be flown into a netherworld where he will name old friends and prevent a judge from being murdered.

I grip my fastened seatbelt and look over at the stolidly humorless soldier and muster a smile that doesn't mask the fact that I'm terrified of sliding out through the open doorway and into the forest. *Trust Dennis,* I admonish myself, trust that I really will be taken to the airport in Letitia for the next flight out to Bogota and home to the good ol' U.S.A.

Only once before have I flown in a helicopter, and that was with Father in a military transport from a U.S. airstrip somewhere near the Caspian Sea back to Tehran for an emergency appendectomy. I was six, and I recall Father holding my hand and my fevered hallucinations. My appendix had ruptured while we were on holiday somewhere near Karaj Dam, a place reputedly holding a nuclear facility today. After my operation I overheard Mother telling dumbfounded ladies at the Officers' Club how a *Persian doctor* had saved me, but it was Father and the U.S. military who'd saved me by getting me to the hospital in Tehran. And now the U.S. is again saving me, and saving Alejandro. I don't doubt the CIA's nefarious work in Colombia, but in the end it was Dennis who we trusted, and it is the CIA that has pulled us out.

I feel a vibrating inside my pocket; my phone, returned to me by Alejandro, and for a heart leaping moment I think he's calling me but when I pull it out I see "ROSIE." The soldier shakes his head "no." Before I slip the phone back into my pocket I see she's left me fifteen messages already. Undoubtedly I'll be given a scolding for leaving her in the lurch with Mother for, *gee, three whole days.*

I have swum with piranhas and sailed under anacondas and slept beside poisonous spiders and hidden from armed cartel thugs and revolutionaries, and while I didn't deliberately choose any of it I can say in retrospect it was a time I will cherish forever and *nothing*, I think, *nothing* Rosie might say to me could impact me more than the past seventy-two hours spent with *mi amor, Alejandro.*

— ◦ —

"Right when you think you've got it all figured out nature throws you a curve ball."

"Mom's had a heart attack," Rosie says in her most recent message of just forty-five minutes ago. "She's in ER and is about to have a cardiac catheterization. I don't know where you are Mira but you have to get here. I really need you to call me."

The moment the chopper lands in Letitia and the soldier has escorted me to the gate for my flight for Bogota, I call, get her voicemail, and leave a message.

"I'm coming, Rosie," I say, "I've been, I've —" I stop before telling her Alejandro took my phone, before confessing I stole Father's ashes and dissolved them into *Lago Tarapoto*. "I'll be there as soon as my flights can get me there," I say.

Dennis has given me a list of do's and don'ts I'm to seriously follow: Don't talk to anyone about what happened. Don't even say you saw Alejandro. Say you never saw him in Cali and you went on to Bogota instead for a little R&R alone. Don't say you were in Letitia. "Tell no one a thing," Dennis said, "Even your family." I wonder how I can follow these instructions, as my family already knew I was flying to Colombia to see Alejandro, then come upon a strategic ploy that relies on Rosie and Mother's overall indifference to anything I do. I will say Alejandro stood me up. Rosie will feel smugly vindicated and I'll simply have to suck it up, the humiliation that isn't real. It will be my first introduction to spy craft, lying to my mother and sister, a taste of what Father must have done for years, and it will be worth it to keep Alejandro safe.

Among the range of people at this small airport on the edge of the wilderness, the backpackers, families, tourists and seedy opportunists, I keep my eyes peeled for Velasco, the man I fear more than any other. I pass my bags through security, my scalp throbbing suddenly with the memory of the pain he inflicted. I worry about my inconclusive ETA since I don't know when my flight arrives into Bogota or what flight I'll be catching to Miami or when the next flight is leaving for Detroit. What must happen, what's been moved back to the top of the list, is: *Hurry home to family, hurry to be with Mother, to help Rosie.*

And while you're at it, don't let the boogey man Velasco nab you.

In a line of passengers crossing the tarmac, I board the 737 up a stairway the old fashioned way. My skin sweats from the damp heat, and while I want relief from it I also know this is the last time I will feel it, that by the time I'm onboard and then in Bogota Airport it will all be circulated air, the humidity and warmth of Colombia no more.

I scan the airstrip for Velasco, but also Alejandro, dreading one man, hoping for one last glimpse of the other. Both are nowhere in sight, and neither is Dennis who, being so tall and American, would be easy to spot. Dennis is escorting Alejandro now and Alejandro is all but under arrest really, and when he boards whatever flight to take him wherever they will take him, he too will take a final breath of the air of his country which he will never see again.

I wonder if Alejandro saw Rosie's messages when he had my phone and if he had chosen not to tell me. No, and yes, and I don't care, is my answer. It isn't my option to accuse him of betrayal; we are done with that. Love is not a game of accumulated points of you did this to me I did that to you.

What I do know is that I am returning home to my country while he is losing his forever.

Hefting my bag into the overhead bin, settling quickly into a window seat, I listen to Rosie's messages, twelve in all, each with increasingly alarming news concerning Mother's condition, from the most current to the first real sign of a serious problem when she fell in the kitchen. I'm shocked by how dramatically Mother has deteriorated in the course of three days, how according to Rosie's messages she began walking sideways, slurring her words, and talking gibberish, possibly due to a stroke. Hospital tests reveal a bump in enzymes, indicating a likely heart attack and evidence of small strokes, and now the upcoming cardiac catheterization will determine whether she'll need heart surgery.

"This is it," says Rosie's final message, "If Mom has to have open heart surgery it doesn't look good. She may not make it. Where are you, Mira? Call us. Mom is asking for you."

Mom is asking for you.

I pull up a text message and am assaulted by a picture of Mother in her hospital bed, IV in arm, face white and frightened. The implication is clear: You have abandoned your mother for a foolhardy romance and now see what's happened to her. Only Rosie would think of sending me such a picture, and only Mother would be willing to pose for it. *This will get Mira's attention*, they must have thought. And it does. Margaret looks pathetic and yet determined, her glasses huge on her pale little face.

They may be impossible, my mother and sister, but they are *my* impossible mother and sister.

Before turning off my phone I leave a second message for Rosie explaining again that I was indisposed. *Indisposed.* What an inappropriate word. Indisposed while Mother was suffering? How could I? How dare I? I am breathless with guilt for having a life-changing experience at what has turned out to be a most inopportune time, for suddenly it's upon us, that impossible realization. It's hard to believe that our mother, the woman who was supposed to be a pain in the ass for the next decade or more, could leave us. Margaret with mini-strokes and heart trouble doesn't fit into the equation of her presumed life course, which for me has always had her living to a feisty cranky ninety-eight like her mother before her.

I check my other messages: Magill says the cats are doing fine, but when will I be coming back, he wants to know; we have three new clients and a house in the Marina that needs "your magical fairyland touch." There's a message from my gynecologist whom I've all but forgotten about, and as I prepare for bad news I'm told instead that I've tested negative on the BRCA for hereditary breast cancer. It's a reprieve. This reprieve tells me to start living again, but how can I live again with Alejandro gone from me forever?

Abre tus ojos, he said, *and someday you will find me.* When will that be, I wonder.

I sleep on the flight to Bogota, sporadically, fitfully, my face turned to the window. I don't dream about Mother but when I awaken I can taste her fear rising like bile in my throat.

When we land in Bogota I call Rosie's cell again, and this time she answers in full-on doc mode. She is factual, calm, incisive. She doesn't accuse me of abandoning her, doesn't ask where I've been or why I haven't called.

"We got your message," Rosie says. Her voice is soft and she's with Mom. They are waiting for her to be taken in for the cardiac catheterization, and although I'm in a plane taxiing down the tarmac to a gate at Bogota Airport, a satellite brings our little triangle of three together — Mother and daughters, bound by blood.

"How is she?" I say.

"Well, she's a bit loopy on Ativan, but here, Mom wants to talk to you."

I hear the rustle and brief confusion of the phone being passed to my mother — *Mommy* — her faint indistinct words. Finally, she is talking to me.

"HI!" Mother says. Tough, vibrant, perky.

"Hey there," I say. The plane has come to a halt and passengers stand up around me, reach for luggage. I too stand while I hang on for dear life, Mother's life, to this connection.

"Sounds like you're undergoing a test," I say.

"Hobson's Choice," Margaret says.

"What's that?" *Perky but loopy*, I think, but then Mother explains.

"That's when you have no choice. That's Hobson's Choice."

God, I'm proud of her. My eyes well with this pride. A disembarking passenger, a casually dressed Latin gentleman, glances my way.

"You'll be fine," I say.

"Yes, well, let's hope so," she says. She speaks carefully and sounds uncharacteristically calm, almost matronly. "I have my personal doctor by my side and she says I'm going to be fine. Here she is —"

Rosie is back on.

"Hi," Rosie says.

"Hobson's Choice, huh? She's tough."

"She's going to be fine," Rosie says. "You're going to be fine," she repeats to our mother.

"She believes you," I say to Rosie, "She always says you never lie to her."

"Yeah." Rosie ruefully catches my meaning. When Mother wanted to know the truth about the fit of a dress, the color of her lipstick or the length of a skirt, she would ask Rosie instead of me, as she knew she would always get the truth instead of kindness.

"Good thing you never lied to her before," I say, "She believes you now."

I too want to believe Rosie, doctor, diagnostician and truth teller. I hear voices in the background, Mother's chirpy voice.

"They're ready for her, we've got to go," Rosie says.

"Okay, later," I say and disconnect.

Soon I'm swept up into Bogota Airport, into the crowds, disoriented by all of it, and for a second my heart speeds up and I'm right there with Mother under anesthesia, drugged, doctors surrounding me, my life in their instruments.

I'm on overload, on the verge of a panic attack. I slip into a sundries store, buy a bottle of water, grab a premade sandwich, slow my breathing, control the surge before it overtakes me. You're just hungry and dehydrated, I say to my inner child. Oh, and you miss your mommy. I wolf down the sandwich while standing in the ticket line and stare at the monitors and the people in clean clothes, abruptly aware of how grungy I look in my filthy cargos. But at least they're J Brand and I'm pulling my Patagonia, which labels me an Extreme Adventurist with money, appearances being everything when wrangling with panic while trying to purchase a last minute ticket bound for home in a foreign city.

As it turns out, Alejandro has bought me an open ended round-trip first class ticket, and so the flight out of Bogota to Miami has me up in the front cabin again. Now instead of rescuing me from a cartel henchman or fending off jaguars, he has wrapped me up in the cocoon of a first class seat bound for home. Nestled in the double-wide chair before take-off, I'm grateful for the little hot hand cloth the attendant passes to me in a pair of sterilized tongs and muse how only hours ago I was slogging through bacteria-infested waters.

I wonder if in this instant Alejandro is thinking of me or if at this moment he's fighting for his very survival. I wonder how I will ever find him again. *You will know how to find me.* His words come back to me now, dropped like a message in a bottle. *You will know how to find me.* But will he want to be found?

The engines whine and increase in pitch and the plane hurls its heavy weight into motion, speeding down the runway, rising up over the land, its interior rustle of people in conversation grown quiet during take-off. I look down on the jungle below me, this place where I've left my father's ashes, where I loved Alejandro de la Torre. I surprise myself with this sensation of my resilience and for a moment I'm awash in guilt for being strong and relatively young, younger than Mother, stronger than Mother, which I don't believe was ever part of her plan.

Deadly Nightshade

"Some people go into hospitals and never come out."

There is no dawn's early light over the squared off fields of corn and parking lots below but rather a swirling darkness as the 757 rocks and rolls down for a landing into wet green Michigan. The wheels slide and skid, but we're here, we're fine, and for the first time in the past twelve hours of flights from Letitia in the Amazon to Bogota and then Miami and now Detroit, it occurs to me I have too much living to do to waste it on fear of flying. Phone back on, I listen to my sister's voice telling me Mother has successfully undergone the cardiac catheterization and won't need heart surgery after all.

"But she's different," Rosie warns in the voicemail, "Be ready."

Wind buffets the airport shuttle as it dutifully plows through sheets of rainfall toward Ann Arbor on a highway littered with the flotsam of wind-whipped trees. We're back in the land of tornados.

"The good news is there's no arterial blockage," Rosie says.

Within the thick corridors of Mercy Hospital we hear no wind or rain, a stunning opposite to the Amazon where just the night before nature and all its insect-sized creatures were slapping against my skin.

Here weather is pictures flashing on TV screens. Gurneys roll by, staffers awaken patients with smells of breakfast; nurses make the morning rounds. As a physician, Rosie is comfortably in her element.

"She's going to have to undergo rehab, you know," she says.

"Rehab? Isn't that another word for nursing home?"

"Mom can't drink anymore, Mira."

"Drink? As in alcohol?"

"Of course alcohol," Rosie says, "It's using up what little's left of her brain cells. She's going to hate me for telling her and she's going to make my life miserable."

"Well, I'm here now and she can blame me."

"How can she blame you when you're her drinking buddy?"

"Drinking relieves her anxiety."

"Well, it was killing her."

I hear, *"you were killing her."*

"You drink with her too, you know."

"The sociologist says we should go to al-Anon. We should also have an intervention."

"So she guzzles wine with dinner and likes a little sherry before bed —"

"Try a lot of sherry. The night after you left I told her she couldn't have any more. She was getting into all kinds of trouble and I'd had it."

"What kind of trouble?"

"I'll tell you later, but just know she was drinking too much and I decided to cut her off."

"So let me get this straight: Because you said she couldn't have sherry before bed she went through withdrawal, had anxiety, her heart started racing and she had a heart attack?"

"Put that way, it sounds like I nearly killed our mother, doesn't it?"

"Murder by detox. What a concept."

Rosie stops in front of the door to Mother's room and lowers her voice.

"I should warn you, she's different," Rosie says.

"Different how?"

"Depressed, I think. Resigned. But she looks great."

As I start to enter she stops me again.

"You really think I tried to kill Mom?"

"Do I have to answer that question?"

Margaret is sitting up in bed and for a moment I don't recognize her. I was prepared to see the shaken woman in my iPhone photo, but looking at her now, you'd never believe she's had a couple mini-strokes in addition to a heart attack and a series of invasive tests. Replenished with IV fluids and off booze for several days, her skin exudes a glow I haven't seen in years and she looks like she's been on vacation. Her daughters meanwhile look like wrecks. Rosie's fashionably cut hair hangs limp around her strained face and I'm still wearing what's become extremely skanky cargos.

"How nice to see you," Mother says. There's no sarcasm in her voice despite the uncharacteristically convivial phrase, and I realize she's struggling to enunciate through the drugs.

"You look great, Mom!"

She registers this with calm indifference then turns back to the TV weather news.

"It's a storm," she says.

"Yes, I just flew into it."

I sit on the edge of her bed and take her unresponsive hand and wait for her to tell me I was lucky my plane didn't crash but she doesn't. We watch the wind and tornado warnings together.

"Here, Mom, have some juice."

Margaret dutifully takes the cup from Rosie and sips. Her eyes are soft and pretty. I see their hazel color, but there is also a void there. How can she look so good and sound so awful? It's as if her personality has been snatched from her body, leaving a placid, attractive face.

"We had a rocky landing," I say, prompting her, "but we made it."

"That's nice," Margaret says. No talk of crash landings or mid-air terrorist attacks. She doesn't exactly smile at me; it's more like she's chosen to be polite. For a moment I wonder if she knows me.

"So how're you doing, Mom?" Another prompt. As in, *I'm your daughter.*

"I want to go home."

Her plaintive tone is almost unbearable. So unlike her, like an old woman, I think; but then, she is an old woman.

"I'm sorry I'm so confused," she says, "I walk into a room and forget why I'm there."

"That's because of the Antivan," Rosie says in all factual certainty, and looks across the bed at me. The Margaret we know has left us.

"Hey, Mom. I brought you some stuff to read," Rosie says. From a canvas bag she pulls out a few magazines and *In Cold Blood*.

"Oooooooh," Margaret says, and reaches for her dog-eared paperback, "I could read this a hundred times. You know it's fascinating that things like that happen."

"Things like that" being two killers breaking into a house and shooting the entire family to death.

Rosie and I look at each other and try not to laugh. She's back.

"What?" Our mother wants to know.

"Nothing," I say, "We can tell you're feeling better."

How did Mother get to be oddly happiest when contemplating ways to die? Had she always been this way or had growing up in wartime on the California coast affect her early adolescence? She'd told us about sea-facing gun emplacements, her fear of "the Japs" invading, but she was also the girl who collected True Detective magazines and fondly poured over grim forensic tales of "unspeakable" crime.

"You could write the book, Mom," Rosie says, "101 Ways Mother Said You Could Die."

"What a wonderful idea," Margaret says, unaware of her sarcasm, "It could be a useful book for all mothers."

We burst into giggles, but Mother doesn't notice. She opens *In Cold Blood* and arbitrarily reads a chapter, any chapter, it doesn't matter, she knows the book by heart.

"Sleep struck him from behind," Mother says, quoting a favorite passage.

She leans back and closes her eyes, the cuddly well-worn paperback rising and falling on her chest.

"Sleep struck him from behind," she mummers again. Apparently it's her sleepy time mantra.

"Leave it to Mom," says Rosie, "To read *In Cold Blood* to help her fall asleep."

On the drive back to her house Rosie launches into a rambling explanation about something I only gradually begin to comprehend. It's about Father's ashes, which seem to be missing, only Mother's the suspect, not me. Indirectly apologetic for having ingloriously shoved the bronze container box on a shelf above the washer, Rosie feels responsible for their disappearance. Just a couple days ago she happened to knock the box over reaching for the "Spray and Wash" and noticed it had a hollow ring.

"Father's ashes are gone, and you know what I think happened?" Rosie says, her gaze fixed on the dark windy stretch of road ahead, "I think our crazy Mother accidentally washed a load with them."

"With Father's remains?"

I don't say *I stole our father's ashes and scattered them in the Amazon.* What I say instead is: "Are you sure?"

"Honestly, Mira! Jonathan's underwear looked dingy, and so did the dishtowels. It's got to be our crazy mother!"

"Do you think Mom's stroke caused her do it?" I ask, thinking, *I'm such a liar.*

"Maybe. But it's just the sort of weird thing she'd do, sort-off accidentally on purpose, acting out some twisted hostility toward Father. That's when I figured she'd been drinking too much, why I cut her off."

Now *I'm* the one who nearly killed our mother. By taking the ashes I unwittingly placed blame on Mom, causing Rosie to cut her nightly sherry intake and prompt her anxiety, alcohol withdrawal, and heart attack.

"Wow," I say. "Then she went through withdrawal, freaked out and had the heart attack. What a way to *almost* die!"

Rosie stops at a light, bends over the steering wheel and shakes with laughter.

"Can you believe it?" she says, "Mom washed our laundry with Father instead of Tide!"

I start with a smirk, but Rosie's laughter is infectious and soon I too am laughing, laughing and crying at the absurd yet entirely credible vision of Margaret in all her nervous impulsive Mom-ness dumping our father's ashes into the top loader.

"Dad in the spin cycle!" Rosie howls.

The image alone is enough to ensure us at least ten more years of psychotherapy.

I don't tell her that Father, the big American in the brown suit, the CIA man with a drawer full of tiny passport photos, ended up swimming with dolphins. I don't think I'll ever tell her, as I'm never one to spoil a good joke with the truth.

　

That night in my basement guest suite, I slip into the bathroom with my phone and call Dennis. It rings and rings and just when I'm about to give up he amazingly picks up.

"Yes," he says. Just that. No identification.

"This is —" I hesitate. He interrupts me.

"I know who this is," Dennis says. He is curt but there's a buttery softness to his voice that is professionally reassuring. I can see his blue eyes, his perfect buzz cut and big shoulders.

"For your friend's sake," Dennis says, "I'm advising you to permanently forget about your friend, do you understand?"

"Is he alright?"

"All threatening parties are about to be taken into custody and no one knows your involvement. And yes, he is." Dennis adds.

"Thank-you," I whisper.

"I strongly advise you to forget your friend," he says again.

"Thank-you," I say, and yet I wait, unwilling to sign off and break the link that brings me closer to him — *he whose name is writ in water.*

"Your welcome," Dennis says without irony and in all politeness ends the connection.

I dream of Alejandro leaving the earth. He is a wisp, a ghost floating up, a whisper of smoke in the air.

I awaken certain he is dead, that something terrible has happened. I look out through the window at the dawning sky and wonder if they miss it, the ones who are truly gone. Do they miss this world? Do they miss the beauty of it? We all die sooner or later, all of us. Death is not negotiable, no matter how we stand guard.

A pale yellow bird, so fleeting and tiny I nearly mistake him for a wayward leaf, alights on a thin twig. He pauses then flutters up into the still wet air. Gone. An escaped canary.

And Alejandro? To where has he escaped?

Meconopsis Betoniciflolia

Or:

Blue Poppy

I say: "You are only afraid of dying if you haven't lived."

It is a brilliantly clear morning in early May and, lo and behold, my next-door neighbor Juanita has lived another year to see her exotic blue poppies bloom. This phenomenal accomplishment is not about her living to be a hundred and one years old but rather about her propagating and growing a rare poppy of this kind – *Meconopsis Betoniciflolia* – the likes of which are seen in such rarified and diverse horticultural environs as London's Kew Gardens and the remote Himalayas.

I stand at my mailbox sifting through bills and my latest copy of *Garden Design* while admiring these blue poppies of hers and the view over my new low picket fence. Juanita waves from her window and I think of how Mother, nearly two decades younger yet unsteady on her feet, no longer walks to my place.

"I'm not as mobile as I used to be," Mother says.

She needn't worry, I assure her. She has her cats and the books she loves to read – *Fatal Vision*, *In Cold Blood*, *Helter Skelter*, anything by Ann Rule – splayed like so many little teepees across her bed where she likes to spend her time reading about misfortune and murder. I've bought her a rolling walker and hired a visiting home care service to deliver meals and remind her to take her medications. Occasionally she'll step outside to look up at Venus sparkling in the early evening sky.

"I find it fascinating," she says these days, "Thinking of how the universe has changed and how it will continue to change."

After I'm gone, I hear.

I sit on my front stoop and open *Garden Design*'s new issue on internationally award-winning landscapes and page through the photographic spread of a beautifully landscaped garden in the Maldives. The garden belongs to the island nation's ecologically outspoken former president who's been warning the international community for some years now about the perils of global warming, yet despite threat of extinction from the rising sea, this lush tropical paradise continues to thrive.

Paging through the article, I admire the garden's water ferns, lotuses, and the exquisite purple blooms of the *siete cueros*. Orchids cascade from trellises, including the unmistakable *Cattleya candida*.

The rare *Cattleya candida* orchid, native of the Cauca Valley of Colombia, land of coca, once clipped from the garden of a *narco traficante* and transported along the Amazon inside a Louis Vuitton bag. Now growing in the Maldives.

Abre tus ojos.

My heart picks up speed, but it isn't a panic attack. It's been a long time since I've had one of those.

Garden Design won't spell it out for me, won't give me a name or picture of his face. I've searched for nearly a year, on the internet, in the news. To this day I hear that voice, see those eyes. Though the man himself has vanished, in my dreams I feel his touch, the hand of the vanishing man.

I read the article carefully but can't find any mention of the landscape architect's name, so I return to the pictures.

A close up of the *Cattleya candida* orchid.

Mira, Miranda. Look and see.

The Maldivian landscape has a distinctive style. There is a trellis with the large orange flowers of the *passiflora parritae* vine. There is a firepit with modern seating. There are giant lily pads floating like emerald stepping-stones upon the surface of a pond.

Amazonia Victoriana.

The style is unique to a gardener whose name has not been spoken since the ceasefire in his country's half-century civil war.

And then I turn the page and see it: In the center of this landscape's glimmering pond is the sculpture of a pink iridescent dolphin rising to meet the sky.

"If you ever swim with dolphins," says the nameless landscape designer, "You will know that you have experienced something truly remarkable."

Abre tus ojos. My eyes are open.

You will know how to find me.

Mira.

Back in the house, I get on the internet and click on Expedia for flights to the Maldives. On Saturday there's an eleven hour, thirty minute flight on Singapore Airlines departing LAX at 3:45 pm, arriving in Tokyo at 7:15 pm, Tokyo time, the following day. After a one hour, thirty-five minute layover, the next flight departs at 8:50 pm, arriving in Singapore at 2:55 am. A seven hour and five minute flight. After another layover of six hours and fifty minutes, the final flight departs Singapore at 9:45 am and arrives in the Maldives' Male International Airport at 11:10 am.

Being my father's daughter, I book the itinerary that will take me on a journey of thirty-one hours and twenty-five minutes of flying and layovers, leaving Los Angeles on the cusp of evening and ending at my holiday destination in the Maldives in the bright light of midday. Being my mother's daughter, I consider the mechanical reliability of aircrafts and ferries in the region, not to mention the pirates. And being just me, Mira Barnes, I trust the fierce clairvoyance of my heart as it opens like the *Meconopsis Betonicifolia* blue poppy, one unfurling petal at a time.

Acknowledgements

This novel wouldn't be what it is without the perceptive editing skills of Natasha Alexis and the kind encouragement from my agent, Jennifer Gates. Susan Dworski's beautiful book cover design gave me impetus to try and live up to her vision, and I'm grateful to Anne Brand Saulnier for talking me down from the "third person" ledge. My sister Cynthia Culler offered memorable anecdotes and our mother Barbara Hyatt contributed as well to the cautionary chapter titles. I'm also thankful for my stepmother Johnye Culler, whose joyful sense of humor aided my perspective. More research than I anticipated went into the Colombia sequences, and for that I'm indebted to Ingrid Betancourt's *Even Silence Has An End*, William C. Rempel's *At the Devil's Table*, Alfred Molano's *The Dispossesed*, Vanity Fair correspondent Maureen Orth's "Inside Colombia's Hostage War," Forrest Hylton's *Evil Hour in Colombia*, Gabriel Garcia Marquez's *News Of A Kidnapping*, Jorge Isaacs' *Maria*, and the inspiring poetry of the incomparable Pablo Neruda.

Finally, I am always and forever grateful for the life I share with my husband Doug Vaughan. We plant seeds in our garden and grow together.